I Found My Heart in San Diego

A Story About Faith, Healing, and The Power of Belief

James M. Vera

America's Leading Inspirational Hypnotist

Jamesmvera.com

ALL ONE PUBLISHING
INTERNATIONAL

First Printing: April 2021

ISBN-978-1-7359947-2-7

All One Publishing International
Miracles Hypnosis Center LLC
142 Elm Street
Cheshire, CT 06410
(203) 490-5100
www.jamesmvera.com

Do you want James M. Vera to be the inspirational speaker at your next event? Call (203) 490-5100 or visit jamesmvera.com.

Why Read This Book

No matter what it is in this life that you are praying for at this moment, it's coming to you, and it's on its way! No matter who you are praying to, "IT" is listening. Just by reading this story you will soon realize that anything is possible. The power of belief is real. The power of your belief is what creates your life. In other words, as soon as you believe "It" is coming, "It" is on the way to manifestation in your physical world. Through your own desire, belief, and expectation, you will manifest your wildest dreams. Regardless of your faith, this story will prove to you that we are all climbing the same mountain. We are all on the same journey. The only difference is we are all taking different paths. I never believed in miracles until I lived through this very story. This is a story about how you can start to truly experience the faith, healing, and power of belief. What is it that you are waiting for? What do you need? Whatever it is, you are worthy and deserving of receiving it. ~ James M. Vera

INSPIRED BY TRUE EVENTS

Acknowledgements

I would like to express love and gratitude to everyone who has made this book a reality. The Universal Higher Power (God) in each of us that allows thoughts to manifest into reality. Maha Lakshmi and Ganapathi for guidance and love. Joey Romain who without his story this book would never have been written. Bella for being a friend and a huge supporter of sharing Joey's message. Jason Linett who planted the first seed about becoming an author on his *Work Smart* podcast. Dr. Richard Nongard whose continued guidance and support is beyond measure, which is what happens when you write a book with Richard. My soul mate and partner of 22 years William Edward who has believed in me even when I didn't believe in myself. My editor and "word shaman" RJ Banks. His ability to convey ideas and make my words dance and sing is like no other. He brings magic to the page. His amazing talent to edit books despite being legally blind shows; RJ Banks is an example of the YES, I CAN attitude. He teaches us his disability is actually his ability. Leo Buscaglia, Dr. Wayne Dyer, Louise Hay, and Dr. Joe Vitale who all taught me that when you change your thoughts your life changes. Baha'u'llah for speaking through Joey Romain to teach me about the power of faith, healing, and the power of belief.

Alwad u adha!

Preface

I wonder if you have ever experienced a chapter in your life that changed you forever? Someone you may have met who had such a huge impact that it changed who you are. A person you feel was sent to you for a reason. I am fortunate enough to be able to tell this story. I was told to tell "the story" I was told to tell it and to tell it often; I was told every time I told "the story" to be sure to mention Baha'u'llah. I will be sure to mention Baha'u'llah and his importance in the story. You will learn just how important Baha'u'llah is in this story. This is how Joey wanted me to tell it. Never did I dream that I would be putting the story in writing. I have told the story to so many of my clients and patients over the years. It has not only impacted me but has also had a great healing effect on most who have heard it! Maybe you are waiting on a miracle? Whatever you are waiting for, it's on its way.

When I began writing my book *Hypnoketosis*, I was looking for inspiration. It seemed like such a big undertaking. I was looking for different types of things I could do spiritually to call in the muses for the inspiration I needed to complete the book. I went on YouTube to look for a meditation which would help me call in my muses.

The guided meditation I listened to was only about 11 minutes long. I shut down my laptop and I sat back in my comfortable office chair and I listened. It was a female voice with wonderful relaxing music in the background. Her voice was soothing and peaceful. I really didn't think I was going to get much out of listening to such a short guided meditation.

She began guiding me through a beautiful meadow with flowers and trees off in the distance. She described the stream that was gently running on the edge of the meadow. Then she said there was a bridge and on the other side of the bridge there was a person walking towards me over the bridge. In my imagination I could see it all so clearly and I felt so peaceful and calm. I saw a man walking towards me. As I continued to see the man coming towards me and over the bridge, I could see a twinkle in his eyes and the happy smile that seemed to take up his entire face. I felt so comforted, almost as if we had met at another time in another place. The man continued to walk towards me and I kept thinking to myself that he looked like the Dalai Lama. The woman's voice then said that I would writing about the person coming across the bridge. I began to chuckle as I thought, "I'm supposed to write about the Dalai Lama? I don't know enough about the Dalai Lama to write a book about him!"

What appeared to be the Dali Lama kept getting closer and closer and as it looked as if the Dalai Lama's smile and face began to morph into my friend Joey. "Oh my God, Joey, is that you?" He answered and said, "Hey Jim, bet you thought I was the Dalai Lama?" Then he erupted into an outburst of hysterical laughter that only my friend Joey Romain and I had shared so many times. An infectious laughter that could get me giggling like I was a kid again.

He said, "Hey kid, tell the story! Tell the story and make sure you mention his name. I told you every time you mention his name and tell this story. He is listening and will grant you all the gifts you could ever want in this life and the afterlife when you meet him again. Remember, I will be waiting there for you as well as all your family and friends and pets." He always said that I could not even imagine for a moment the infinite number of gifts that you could receive just by mentioning his name.

Joey was a man of great faith and belief. He was not a religious man by any means. Not pious in any way. Not a saint, just an angel in disguise. We are all sent angels in this life and I was sent one of the biggest gifts I have ever been given. After meeting Joey, I realized there are certainly no coincidences in life and everything happens for a reason. The Universe is in perfect synchronicity at all times. Just like Edgar Cayce talks about in the Akashic Records, all is pre-planned with the ability of free will to change the trajectory at any time. I think there were times as this story was unfolding that I took it for granted like we often do with people we meet. Hindsight being 20/20, I can see perfectly clear this was my time to learn about faith, healing, and the power of belief.

This friendship was sent, and it was different than any other friendship I had ever had before or have ever had since. He was a friend who was sent to bring me lessons and messages. I also realize that each person that comes into our lives has been sent with a lesson. This felt special. This was different than so many others who had come into my life before him. There were times when the message was unspoken and there were other times when it was direct. My favorite messages from Joey were the ones that came with laughter. There was plenty of laughter. Mostly very slapstick which I did well with having spent many hours with my grandfather who shared the same type of silly slapstick humor. Silly Jokes like: There was a grasshopper who came into a bar. He hopped up on the bar stool and the bartender said, "Hey did you know we have a drink named after you?" The grasshopper said "What, you have a drink named Irving?" And then he would break into the biggest belly laugh with tears nearly running down his face. It was contagious and before I knew it, I was laughing so hard. To most others, there was nothing that funny about that cornball humor, but Joey had that way to make you laugh over the simplest things.

There were many times of laughter, serious moments, and tearful moments as Joey was able to guide me through an incredible journey which has taught me almost everything I know about faith, healing, and the power of belief.

I was raised Roman Catholic and attended parochial high school. I hated every moment of it and at the same time I am now grateful for the foundation it gave me. With all the religious ceremonies over the years I attended in high school and a lifetime of Catholic Church, I never understood faith. I never understood that within each and every one of us there is our own Infinite Spirit which dwells deep within our souls. Our own personal Christ within. I did have one special priest in my life, Fr. James Chichetto C.S.C, author of *All for Her: The Autobiography of Fr. Patrick Payton*. Fr. Jim, as he was often called, was a great influence on me; he was able to instill a bit of belief and faith in me, however, I spent most of my years begging God instead of knowing that what I asked for was already given freely. I believed in a judgmental and punishing God. I am sure Fr. Jim would be quite surprised to know that I am not only a believer but an author as well.

Nothing would compare to what I was about to learn from spending the wonderful gifted hours I was given to be with my dear friend Joey. I call them gifted hours because in retrospect I see that every hour was a gift from Infinite Spirit to help me along my journey. Each hour spent learning seems like it was wrapped in gold sparkled wrapping. Each moment was presented with a huge gold bow on top.

These lessons occurred with no effort. He would lead often by example or share a story or an anecdote of his own experiences to prove a point. Each and every visit was filled with the love, laughter, joy, and warmth you could only experience with an angel. The smile, the twinkle in his eyes. He had a charisma and could light up a room. Everybody wanted to be around Joey. His hair was as white as a fresh winter snow. I just had a chuckle thinking how he and I shared our disdain for snow and cold climates. He grew up in upstate NY Poughkeepsie and would always say that snow and leaves never made any sense to him. He would ask why you would live in a place where you have to shovel snow all winter and then rake leaves all fall and sweat through the summer and then do it all over again the next year. He'd say, "What's wrong with those people? Why would they keep wanting to do that year in and year out?" We met in San Diego in 1998 and agreed that it was the finest weather and didn't know why anyone would want to live anyplace like the Northeast.

One of the ironies is that I am telling this story from the Northeast. If I were to complain about living here, I could just hear his voice telling me. "Jim you never know when Baha'u 'llah is going to call you or where you will have to go. If you are there you are meant to be there for a reason." He would also tell me that some people come into our lives for a short time and others come for a lifetime but they all come with a message and it is not for us to ask why they come or why they go.

People are in your life just long enough for you to learn what it is that you are supposed to learn.

As I was writing this preface, I was interrupted by a call but I hit decline and kept typing. Two minutes later, again the phone rang. I was concerned so I looked and it was two calls from Poughkeepsie, NY. This gave me a chill as that is where the story began as that is where Joey is from. I listened to the two voice messages and they both said, "It's Ruth. Please don't come to Poughkeepsie tonight - it's too late." I decided to break from writing and called Ruth to tell her she had the wrong number. I asked why she was dialing a number with a Connecticut area code, and she replied, "That's strange, I was trying to call my plumber back and hit redial." How my number showed on Ruth's redial I will never understand except to say that I know that is the biggest indicator for me to "tell the story!"

Join me now in a story of how miracles really do happen. Miracles are happening to you all the time. It is a matter of taking the time to live a simple life and stop long enough to notice the wonders. No matter what your religious upbringing or beliefs, the power of belief is what allows you to see the manifestation of miracles in your life. This is not just a story about me meeting my mentor, friend, and muse, this is a story about how when you believe, anything is possible. Anything is possible! When you truly believe, you can create the life you want and turn tragic moments into times of healing, growth, and faith. It's your turn to benefit from this miraculous story. Miracles follow miracles and wonders shall never cease. I Found my Heart in San Diego and that is how I learned about faith, healing, and the power of belief. Now, it's your turn!

Table of Contents

CHAPTER 1

Our story begins in the year 1955 in Poughkeepsie, New York. Marilyn Monroe was gracing the silver screen in *The Seven Year Itch*, *The Honeymooners* were all the rage on TV, and "Rock Around the Clock" was the number one song in the country. From around the corner, screeching the tires of his Chevy Bel Aire Convertible, David pulled up to the curb in front of a house. A young man, Joey Romain hopped into the car and the boys quickly whisked away. With Bill Haley and his Comets blaring from the metal dash board speaker, Joey stood up, and with his two middle fingers raised, he yelled at the top of his lungs, "FUCK YOU…FUCK YOU!" This was very unusual for a young man who was rarely heard saying any curse words, but now was the time. After years of being the victim of an abusive and drunken father, Joey Romain had finally made his escape! It was a bittersweet moment for him as he watched his Italian mother crying as they sped away, and his drunk father yelling "FUCK YOU… FAGGOT!" and giving the middle finger back. Joey's little sister Bella, who was nine years younger, stood, hanging onto her mother, crying, heartbroken, and sobbing that she wanted her Joey back.

Joey was born Joseph Alexander Pabisinski in May of 1937. I would not know this was his real name until many years later. I knew him as Joey Romain. I learned that he changed his name when he got into the hair business in the 1950s. He said he went to a movie with his friend Sam and he saw the name as a director in the film. He thought it sounded better for a hair stylist to be named Joseph Romain instead of Joseph Pabisinski. Joey took to the scene in the 1950s and grew up fast. He was on the shorter side, about 5'7", and always believed in working out so he was always defined and toned. He was very handsome and wanted to be a model; however, due to his height that wasn't in the cards for him. I often wondered if that was why he enjoyed being around the glamour business. It didn't matter if it was a person, a room, or a building, Joey could make a five-dollar item look like it came from Neiman Marcus. He just had a knack and an eye for color fashion design and the latest trends.

Joey had an uncle, his mother's brother, who lived in Manhattan. Joey would take the train from Poughkeepsie into Grand Central Station, where his uncle would be waiting for him. He would be sure he had a nice suit for Joey to change into and that Joey was dressed like royalty. He would take Joey to the finest restaurants in Manhattan and teach him table manners and fine dining. He would also take him to some of the best plays on Broadway. Joey loved the finer things and absorbed, like a sponge, the culture he was being taught by his uncle. Joey said it was an escape for him away from the continued emotional and physical abuse he endured from his father.

His father had changed a little bit after Bella was born. Being nine years younger, she lived a better life than Joey, and thank God her father never put a hand on her. In fact, she was daddy's little girl! Sadly though, she would spend many years of her life feeling guilty that Joey had been so abused. She would tell me years later that some of Joey's beatings were pretty bad, and may had affected him with some cognitive functions later on in life. Joey and Bella were very close as brother and sister even though there was nine years of difference. I often admired their relationship as it was just the opposite for me and my own sister. I always wished I had in my sister what he had in Bella. He would tell me how he was like a father to her. He would change her diapers and take care of her so his mom could keep house. He said he would take Bella with him to the dump and find old furniture and turn things into gems. I think that is where his love of antiques, flea markets, swap meets, and garage sales came from.

He told Bella for many years the reason why he didn't want kids was because of her. He would say, "I already had a kid. It was you!" He told me he wasn't a big fan of having children. He said he liked kids; they just weren't for him. He told me someone once said to him, "Joey, some day you are going to wake up and wish you had kids." In one of our philosophical conversations about life one day, he said to me with a big Joey laugh, "Jim, I woke today and I am 64 years old and I still don't regret not having kids," giggling the entire time. "Nope hasn't happened yet."

He was always proud to mention that he was a Taurus and held true to the traits of a Taurus. He was into astrology and many of the other mysteries of the Universe. His mother was a sweet little Italian lady who married a mean Polish alcoholic. He spent years abusing Joey and his mother, both physically and mentally. When Joey spoke of his mom it was always about her Italian cooking and how sweet she was. When he spoke of his father it was with extreme hatred. Joey was so chill and relaxed that there wasn't much that brought that side of him out. He seldom brought up his father as it was definitely a trigger. He in fact told me that when his father died, he would celebrate. A Taurus true to his stubborn bull nature, he did in fact celebrate and had a toast with a margarita poolside with Bella in Florida many years later. He was laughing delightfully when he told me the story and how he proclaimed, "HALLELUJAH…. THE MOTHERFUCKING BASTARD IS FINALLY DEAD!" as they toasted.

Joey never identified as gay or bi or any label. He simply had people he had affairs and relationships with. David was Joey's first boyfriend. He was five years older than Joey. They had great times together as David happily introduced him to this fun and adventurous lifestyle. Joey described David as "all man" with James Dean looks and a Marlon Brando toughness and confidence about himself. Joey adored David and looked up to him. They had a great deal of fun together. One of their favorite "fun" spots was Fire Island. Located next to Long Island, Fire Island was a very exclusive and popular party spot amongst the gay community back then. As a 15-year-old boy Joey would sneak off to Fire Island with David in the summer and would often be found dancing on the table tops, shirtless, and getting a lot of attention from all the guys that were more than happy for the entertainment.

David knew of the horrible situation at Joey's home, and offered to take him, his mother, and Bella away from the nasty and abusive circumstances. In the years to follow the only thing negative Joey would ever say about his mother was that she made the wrong decision when she chose to stay instead of taking Bella and coming west with him and David. Joey had spent weeks trying to talk his mom into escaping with them and starting a new life in California. He promised her he could help her take care of Bella and they could start over without the horrifying abusiveness of his father.

On the road, he and David had a great ride across America. Back then you could drive the original Rout 66 from NY all the way to California. This was in 1958, before the major interstate system was put in place. He said he and David laughed and sang along with the hits on the radio along the way, and they had a wonderful time together. He said because David resembled James Dean so much, that when they were traveling across the country he would look over at David and admire his good looks. He felt like he was in a James Dean movie.

David and Joey arrived in Oakland, California, just across the bay from San Francisco. They stayed with an aunt of Joey's while they looked for jobs. As with many stories though, there was a plot twist. Just when you think they're going to live happily ever after; it is revealed that there is an underlying problem. The problem was that David loved to drink excessively, and this was working on Joey's nerves. He was obviously not a fan of alcoholics like his father and he saw the writing on the wall for him and David. He was in a pickle because they lived with Joey's aunt and Joey was never the type to want to make a scene. He was not one to air his dirty laundry, as they say.

It wasn't long after they arrived at his aunt's that the two had to go their separate ways. Joey had a great attitude about relationships and viewed them as lasting as long as they were supposed to last. In fact, he used to say, "Once the bed is turned down the same way every time with a towel and lube on the nightstand in the exact same place, the same scene over and over again, that's when this Taurus is ready to move on." He never liked the routine of steady relationships. He found it to be so boring after a while. Joey loved adventure and when it came to relationships, he was ready for a change.

Joey would find jobs as a window decorator for some of the finer furniture stores in the Bay Area. He learned a lot about interior design and color while he worked for some of the major department stores at that time like Brunner's and Hales Department stores. He would hustle with the window decorating and use the money to put himself through school to become a hairstylist.

CHAPTER 2

Bella had just turned 17 and decided she wanted to give it a go in California. She had been dating a young gentleman in Poughkeepsie, on and off, and was wanting to settle down. He, on the other hand, was a handsome young man enjoying living a youthful, adventurous, party lifestyle with no interest in a commitment or settling down. Joey said, "Hey sis, why don't you come out here to Cali with me?" Bella had just finished beauty school in Poughkeepsie and was excited to start her new adventure as a hairstylist. Bella arrived at the Greyhound bus station in LA with nothing but what she was wearing. Sadly, all her clothes had been stolen and she was literally starting with nothing. Thankfully some of Joey's friends were kind enough to gather a few things for her to wear.

Bella had a challenging time at first, not only adjusting to California life, but to her older brother's lifestyle as well. Joey was living life in the fast lane, working hard by day, partying the night away, then getting up and doing it all over again. They had rented a house together in Lake Merritt. A 9-room house for $75. Once settled, Bella and Joey opened up a successful hair cutting place right on the Alameda Army Base.

After almost two years living in California, though, Bella was not really enjoying the fast-paced life. She sensed it was difficult for Joey to be himself with his younger sister around. She was also wanting to go back to Poughkeepsie to give her relationship with Derrick one more chance. Derrick was four years older than Bella and was doing everything he could to get her to come back to Poughkeepsie. After many discussions with Joey, they decided to closed the Alameda shop. Joey would resume his career at another salon in town, and Bella would return back to Poughkeepsie where she would marry Derrick, have two boys of her own, and enjoy a lifelong loving relationship with her husband and family who she treasured.

Joey was always a very hard worker and he continued to work designing windows in Oakland. It was at one of the departments stores that he would meet who would become his nearest and dearest friend in his whole life. He met Sam. They soon became the best of friends. He described Sam as the brother he never had. Sam was a handsome Greek young man with a beautiful body. He had dark hair and thick black hair and olive skin. Joey said Sam had an energy that surrounded him that was captivating, enchanting, and catchy. Sam, his sister Jenny, and Joey would enjoy many adventures together.

With Bella now happily back in Poughkeepsie, Joey's partying lifestyle kicked into high gear! Vladimir and Alina were an eastern European couple that lived next to Joey (and Bella) in Lake Merritt. They were highly educated and were both professors. Just before Bella left to go back home, she told Joey she had a funny feeling about Alina and her husband, and to be careful and not to trust them. Their friendship with Joey would get to be a close bond over the next couple of years. He would remain friends with them during his friendship with Sam and Jenny. On the weekends, Joey, Sam, Jenny, Alina, and Vladimir would often head down to Laguna Beach and go water skiing. Joey loved to water ski. He told a story of how he almost drowned one time in Laguna. He and the gang were taking turns driving the boat and water skiing. Joey was on the skis and the others were partying and not paying attention when they looked back and saw Joey had been dragged under the water and was unable to right himself back on his skis. They were able to get him to shore and pump the water out of his stomach and revive him. He was truly the man who had more than nine lives. Unfortunately, as Bella had predicted, his relationship with Vladimir and Alina would also prove to be one of the worst situations in his life.

Joey and Sam would start to hang around together after they got finished at the store. Sam would show Joey the value of working out and taking care of his body. He showed Joey how to work out and they went to the gym back in the day when it was not popular. Sam would later introduce Joey to the late Jack Lalane. Jack was a fitness guru of the 1950s and 1960s. Joey and Sam would work out with Jack and later on Joey would become friends with both Jack and his wife Elaine. Joey was often on the fringe of famous people. They were just people to Joey; he was not in awe of their stardom.

Sam was like a brother to Joey. He took Joey under his wing and introduced him to his mom and sister and the entire family. Although Joey admired Sam, he said they never had romantic interests. He described the relationship to be like brothers. They became extremely close and he became one of the adopted members of Sam's family. Sam's mom owned a beauty school and she convinced Joey and Sam to become hairstylists. Sam knew how lucrative the hair business could be after watching his family. It was the beginning of the 1960s when there were all types of crazy doo's and chemical process being done. This meant for every service extra you were able to do, the more money you would make.

Sam and Jenny's parents were very wealthy and owned many shopping strip plazas in the Bay Area. In one of their plazas was Bayview Beauty College. Both Joey and Sam quickly enrolled and were excited to begin their newest adventure together. Joey insisted on paying his tuition and would work as many hours as he could designing windows and then head over to the beauty school. He even took on a job cleaning the school at the end of the day so he could help to pay down his school tuition faster.

He said every member of his new Greek family drove new Cadillacs, and they were sure to treat Joey as a son so every two years, he would get his "own cad" to drive around in. He was treated very well by this Greek family, and they treated Joey like one of their own children. They spent holidays together and Sam's family became Joey's family of choice. He did also keep in touch with his mom and Bella through the mail and an occasional phone call.

Joey enjoyed learning all about how to make women look more beautiful. He used to love to pick out clothes for his mother and sister. He really loved all the groovy hairstyles of the 1960s with the updo's and all the color and chemical treatments you could do with hair. One day Sam and the rest of the family were sitting around the table with Joey enjoying a nice Sunday meal when they started to tease him about his polish name. They told him he should come up with something that was easy to pronounce. They loved his first name Joseph but said he needed to change the last name. That was when he and Sam ventured off to an afternoon matinee to see a foreign movie. Joey loved the name of the director, Antonio Romain. From that day forward, Joey Pabisinski transformed into Joey Romain until the day he was laid to rest.

Joey picked up doing hair as a natural, and his personality was perfect for the business. He was gentle, and kind, entertaining, a good listener, and boy oh boy could this man work miracles with hair! Both women and men loved him. He began to notice that he was a magnet to people, and they were all attracted to him. He spent his time going back and forth between department stores and doing hair and gaining clients. Joey was a natural for the finer things as a result of his trips going into Manhattan and learning from his uncle who was a connoisseur, or "bachelor" of the finer things life had to offer. I wonder if the words "Bachelor" and "Old Maid," or "Spinster" were code words for Lesbian and Gay back when it was still underground. His uncle would take Joey to plays and fine restaurants. Joey was exposed to the current trends and fashion of the 50s on these trips into New York and seeing all the wonderful window displays in Macy's and Saks and Bloomies.

Soon, Joey had a huge clientele list at the hair salon and was able to leave the window designing behind to do hair full time. He would spend a couple years working for his new family and enjoying all the perks, such as a new Cadillac every two years. Joey was interesting because he would always let others show him the way. He never worried about how financing worked or how things were getting paid for. The details of those things totally escaped him. As long as somebody was working out the details he was all set. I remember him telling me he had a female hair client who was a real estate agent and she would do all his real estate deals for him. All he would have to do is sign when it was time to do the closing and title transfers. He had this amazing ability to allow others to do it all for him and find honest people to lead him through the process.

It was now the early 1970s and disco was starting to be a thing! As you may have guessed, Joey and Sam were right in the middle of the scene with their silk shirts and leisure suites. Joey loved to dance and said that he was quite the dancer. They would work hard and play harder. He and Sam would do hair all day, go the gym for a quick workout and shower, then hit the clubs over on the Castro. The Castro area was one of the first gay communities in the country and "THE" place to see and be seen. Everyone always looked forward to seeing Joey and Sam out at the clubs as they were often the "life of the party!" They enjoyed dancing the night away at the Trocadero Transfer. The Trocadero Transfer was an after-hours dance club in San Francisco from its opening in December 1977 to the late 1990s. It was located at 520 4th Street. Ironically, I was there years later on their last night of being open on a New Year's Eve. I had never seen anything like it before. The place was wild. The Studio 54 of San Francisco for a great comparison. Cocaine was becoming popular at the clubs and it was a way to keep going all night at the clubs, but also a way to stay up while they cut hair all day and worked out at the gym. Sam was getting more and more into coke and he, Joey, and many people viewed it as harmless, like caffeine in coffee. Just a pick me up. Joey started to worry about Sam living in the fast lane, working on properties, doing hair, and burning the party candle all night long.

Sam was also wheeling and dealing in Real Estate in San Francisco in addition to the hair business. He purchased a large apartment building in San Francisco and told Joey they were going to be partners on the building. Sam moved into the building as did his sister Jenny. With Sam's assets growing larger and larger, he drew up paperwork to make sure Joey was taken care of if he passed before Joey. In fact, Sam's parents would often tell Joey he was their adopted son and would share in their wealth when they passed.

It was now the late 70s and Sam was spending most of his time working on the building now. He and Joey would only see each other on the weekends, or when they worked together on one apartment or another within the building. They were both extremely busy with their own lives and projects and it was not unusual for days to pass without talking. After almost a week of not talking, Joey was getting quite concerned. He would call Sam's apartment several times but get no answer. Remember this was the late seventies and there were no cell phones. Finally, he called over to a person that lived in the building and found out that Sam was found unresponsive and rushed to the hospital a couple of days back. Soon after, he finally received a call from Jenny telling him that Sam was gone. He had died of cocaine-induced cardiac failure. Joey felt so betrayed. Who wouldn't? How could Sam do this to him? How could Sam treat his body like that and abuse drugs leaving Joey stranded in life. This was a huge, painful loss that Joey did not have the ability to handle. He said for the next five years he would "bunk into himself." I always assumed this meant that he was bumping into himself because he was so lost. Unfortunately, this was not going to be the last time that Joey was going to be "bunking into himself."

It wasn't long before Jenny stopped returning Joey's calls. She acted like she didn't know Joey. He was hurt and devastated that not only did he lose his best friend, but also the woman who he called his sister. He found out that there was no will and that Jenny inherited everything. Their parents had died a couple of years earlier as well, leaving Jenny to inherit it all but she never gave Joey one red cent. This was just another one of those moments he described in his life, saying, "Jim, I could walk down this driveway with just the clothes on my back and rebuild all over again." He had done it so many times in his life and always had the faith and belief that everything was going to be ok.

He continued to see Alina and Vladimir as it really helped to lessen the pain about losing Sam. It was a great time for them to seize on the moment of Joey's grief. A time when he was the most vulnerable he had ever been in his life. It wasn't long after Sam's passing when Vladimir and Alina invited Joey over for dinner to discuss a business venture. Joey was always interested in ways to make money so they thought they would share the opportunity. Joey was bright, but at the same time he often had the naivety of a young curious teenage boy. They told Joey that their friends, who lived in Columbia, would be mailing the *Time* and *Life* magazines. The job was quite simple: Joey would get the magazines at a post office box and drive them down to Los Angeles to various addresses of wealthy friends of Alina and Vladimir. Joey loved Los Angeles and really enjoyed riding with the top down in his Cadillac with the ocean breeze and his favorite tunes blasting on the radio. Riding the 101 was one of his favorite rides. I laugh thinking about it because he had a horrible sense of direction and was clueless with a map. God knows how he ever found any place he was looking for with no GPS back then.

At first, they led Joey to believe that it was secret important documents that were rolled up in the pages of the magazines. Joey was highly paid to run the magazines to Los Angeles After several months of delivering the "classified magazines," he was making a delivery and recognized a high-profile actor. The celebrity was very friendly and invited Joey in and offered him a drink. There were several other people he recognized in the living room in Malibu overlooking the gorgeous blue water of the Pacific. They were people who he had seen on a couple of the day time talk and game shows of the time. The funny thing about Joey is, as often as he brushed his elbows with fame, it never phased or impressed him. This drop was unusual though because this time he was invited in to hang out and mingle. He noticed the man he delivered the magazine to had disappeared from the party for quite some time. He also noticed several of the guests heading to the back of the house and then coming back. Finally, one of the guests came up to him and said, "Hey man, Blankety-Blank is giving out lines in the back if you want some. He just got a fresh batch from Columbia and it's pure fucking snow." At that moment it all became clear to him exactly what was going on. He was also concerned because Alina and Vladimir were very involved in his life and he was beginning to feel he was in too deeply into a situation he wouldn't get out of easily.

When he got back to the Bay Area, he confronted Vlad and Alina in a diplomatic way as only Joey knew how, and asked them why they didn't tell him what was going on. They claimed they thought he knew and that that the word "classified" was a code word for the coke. They told him they were now receiving it in toothpaste tubes and the entire operation was much safer. He would also get paid triple what he was getting for the magazines. As he would say later, these are the things we learn in life. These are lessons. It became comfortable for him to do this once or sometimes twice per month. He did keep thinking in his mind that his sister Bella had warned him about these two when they first met.

CHAPTER 3

Joey continued to visit his high-profile clients and deliver them their "toothpaste." He even became a regular at several different homes. Unfortunately, unbeknownst to him, he was being watched and followed by the FBI, the DEA, and the LAPD, as were Alina and Vlad. The feds moved in and shut down the operation, and Joey found himself behind bars in the Los Angeles County jail. With no one to call, he felt stupid and alone. There was no Sam to call, and he didn't want to call Bella right away. He knew that if he did call her there would be several "I told you so's." Unable to raise enough money for bail, he remained in the Los Angeles county jail for several weeks. While he was in jail, he said three men from Tijuana had raped him. He said they put razor blades onto popsicle sticks and held them up to his throat while the others took turns sodomizing him. He feared for his life. He said it was one of the most traumatic things he had ever experienced. He eventually was able to hire a decent lawyer and post bail with the condition that he work and live in Los Angeles until the trail was completed. Joey continued to pray to Baha'u'llah and apologize for his errors. He made a deal with Baha'u'llah that if he was able to help him out of this situation, he would never sell or be involved with cocaine or drugs ever again. Joey didn't consider pot a drug, nor did he sell it; he just loved to smoke it.

Joey also believed that the reason why he never contracted HIV or the AIDS virus was because his experience in jail traumatized him to any type of receptive anal intercourse. We now know this is one of the main ways the virus is transmitted. Joey was different in the way that he never really identified as gay. He enjoyed sex with both women and men even though most of his sexual encounters were with men. Like most Taurus men, he was hard to pin down for long-term commitment. He was never big on routines that lasted for too many years. "They just become too boring," he would boast with a mischievous grin reminiscent of the Cheshire Cat.

Joey said he could always get up and go and leave with just the clothes on his back and start over in a new city at any time. And that is exactly what he did. Moving to Los Angeles would create an entirely new life for Joey.

He always believed in the fact that everything always works out. He found himself a cute studio apartment and settled into his new life, new city, and new opportunities. He was concerned that he was still being watched by the Feds so he didn't want any roommates that could get him into issues with his probation.

Because of Joey's charisma, it wasn't long before he landed a full-time job at The Beverly Hilton. Back in those days the male hairstylists were required to do hair in tuxedos. He used to laugh and tell me his name at the Beverly Hilton was Mr. Joseph. It was very formal with many of the stars of the day coming in. As I have mentioned before, Joey wasn't really impressed with the "who's who" of Hollywood, and treated everyone the same. He said he would have to apply all the chemical dyes and perm treatments of the day without getting any on his tux. He blended very well with the people there and made friends. In fact, he said at Christmas time he would have to be careful which party invitations he refused and which ones he went to, as not to offend anyone. He always said he loved people, but they were energy suckers and he needed his quiet and down time to recharge his batteries every now and then.

He had various stars who were his regular clients and was often invited to their homes. He kept a scrapbook of all the notes the people had given him over the years. One of his favorite actresses was Elsa Lanchester, who played the bride of Frankenstein in the 1935 film named as such.

Even though he was not starstruck, he was impressed by some of the stars of his youth and held them in high esteem from back in the day when his uncle was teaching him the finer things in life and the various music entertainers of the day. He loved music from different eras, but he especially enjoyed the days of Rosemary Clooney and the Rat Pack. Being Italian, he could identify with all the music of his early youth.

In his later years he would often reminisce about how he began to do Rosemary Clooney's hair at the Beverly Hilton Salon, and he became friends with her. One day she invited Joey over to her house to have lunch. She gave him the address, which was 1019 Roxbury Drive in Beverly Hills. He knew that she was married to Jose Ferrer, who was a Puerto Rican actor, theater & film director so he was excited to find the house. Being new to Los Angeles, he didn't realize at the time that that was the street to live on in Beverly Hills. Jimmy Stewart and Lucille Ball were her neighbors.

It was a beautiful, sunny southern California day when Joey pulled up to 1019 Roxbury Drive in his Cadillac with the top down. He walked up to the front door and rang the bell. Having made countless deliveries to celebrities in the past, he was expecting a maid or a butler to greet him at the door. As he was waiting, he could hear a bunch of kids yelling, screaming, and playing by the pool in back yard. He also heard a woman yelling, "Now all you damn kids settle down and knock it off… Go out in the pool and play, and no Goddamn running and jumping all over the fucking house!" Finally, someone came to answer the door. Much to his surprise and shock, it was Rosemary herself just looking like any other woman with a house full of crazy kids running around. He said any pedestal she was on came right down to earth that day. He said the kids that were running around that day were her nieces and nephews, including little George. He had a wonderful lunch with Rosemary, and they became close friends.

While having to stay in Los Angeles as part of his bail agreement, he made a life for himself. He said he would keep himself very busy working at the Beverly Hilton salon. He had to be there for a year or more, so he chose to make the best of it. He loved to go see live music and enjoyed the music scene and made a lot of friends. His court date finally arrived and Joey, if convicted, was possibly facing many years in the federal prison system. Once the trial began and was in session, he noticed there was whispering between his lawyer and the prosecution. They asked to approach the bench to speak with the judge. After a very short conversation at the bench, they took the meeting into the judge's chambers. Joey said the minutes seemed like hours waiting for them to emerge back into the court room. Apparently, there was an issue with the possibility of someone tampering with the evidence. He was cleared, released, and ready to return back to the Bay Area.

He believed that Baha'u'llah made this happen so Joey kept his promise for the rest of his life. He never touched coke ever again, nor did he want to associate with anyone who had anything to do with cocaine. He had done it on a rare occasion himself and never understood why anyone would do it. Given the fact that cocaine is what killed Sam, he said he surprised himself that he would have ever gotten involved. This is how Joey taught. He would share an experience through stories. In this particular story, he explained to me that, when you ask Baha'u'llah for something, he hears you and understands what you need and why you are asking for it. He would also impress upon me the need to believe it was coming and that it already happened.

It was now nearing the end of the 70s and things were changing with the times. It was now time for Joey to return back to San Francisco, the city he loved most. Upon his return he quickly learned that women were moving away from the up do's and dye jobs they had been spending big money on. The trend now was the shorter styles like the "shag" and a "pixie" like Twiggy. It made no sense to Joey, and there was no creativity in it at all, but it did give him a new business idea, men's hair!

He sold his houses in Mt. Claire and rented an apartment over a store front close to the Castro. He opened a high-end men's barber shop in the store front and was charging $25 for a man's haircut in the 1970s which was a big price at that time. It was a one-person shop just him by appointment only. He made a good name for himself as a barber and he also loved his female dyke clients, as he would say. They were wonderful customers and he loved all his people from the community. He had a variety of clients both men and women and not just gay clients; people from all over the city would come to get a haircut from "The One and Only" Joey Romain.

"The Tree House" is what everyone called Joey's apartment above the barber shop. It was surrounded by huge eucalyptus trees and it gave the appearance that he lived in a tree. The fresh smell of eucalyptus would be throughout the apartment. Peter Wilton would talk about going over and seeing Joey at the Tree House and he would walk up the back stairs and hear Paul McCartney and Wings Band on the Run playing. Joey would offer him a puff off the joint he usually lit up as you walked in and then pour you a nice glass of Carlos Rossi Burgundy. He said a joint and a class of Carlos Rossi were almost as good as dark chocolate and red wine. Years later when I would visit Joey on 35th street in San Diego he turned me onto the combination of a glass of Carlos Rossi and a joint. At that time, he was more into listening to the Rat Pack and Rosemary Clooney than Paul McCartney. He would never turn down an opportunity to blast some Bill Withers "Lovely Day!" Every day for Joey Romain was a lovely day because he believed everyone is in charge of making it a lovely day regardless of their circumstances. He was a true believer in making lemonade out of lemons.

Although he loved his routine, Joey was getting tired of the hair business. He would cut hair all day, go bar hopping and dinner with friends, and then finish the night at what he called "The Tubs." Those were the gay bath houses of San Francisco. Joey said he was called "Queen of the Vapors" because friends would see him there so often. He also liked the entertainment because back in those days they had acts like Bette Midler and other comedians that were getting started. Performing to a bunch of men in towels, as Bette Midler would say. He would often say if he never had the razors held to his throat in Los Angeles that he maybe would have contracted HIV and died of AIDS like so many of his friends of the time.

Joey began to get interested in architectural painting on the high-end homes up and down the coast of California. He worked with Frank Lloyd Wright's grandson and learned some cool ways to paint the interiors and exteriors of buildings. He started slowly cutting back his days cutting hair and would instead spend them rolling paint. Joey's father was a painter and he worked with him when he was a kid so he had an understanding of how to roll paint. He said after all the years of cutting hair this was a refreshing change.

One of his first jobs was a large painting of an interior down in Los Angeles. The money he was going to be paid was worth it. The home was owned by an Italian filmmaker who wanted to redo the look of the inside of this great home in the hills of Los Angeles He told Joey that he would hardly ever be around but that his girlfriend Donna would be there to let him in.

As expected, when Joey arrived Donna answered the door. She said, "Hello, you must be Joey and have come here to paint the place." Joey asked for her boyfriend and she said he was in Europe but they were looking forward to him getting started on the place. Joey said there was something magnetic about Donna and he was immediately drawn to her. Because Joey was also very charming and charismatic, Donna and Joey hit it off while he was painting and working around the property. They were becoming the best of friends. She went on to explain that the relationship she was in was very lonely. She said basically her boyfriend wanted a pretty model-type girl on his arm to take to Hollywood parties and that was the extent of the relationship. She was so lonely and loved Joey's sense of humor.

One day Donna offered Joey a cigarette and some coffee. He said he sat there with her talking and it was as if they had known each other forever. He never smoked before other than weed, but he really enjoyed the combination of the cigarette and coffee. She was lonely and so was he. He got back to painting and she offered him lunch, some left-over cold meatloaf to make sandwiches with. He said he loved cold meatloaf and she agreed, saying she thought she was the only one who loved cold meatloaf. They began each morning with a cigarette and a coffee and then met again for lunch in the living room to eat cold meatloaf sandwiches and watch old black and white movies.

Donna's boyfriend of convivence loved the house so much that he asked Joey if he would consider painting his other house in Santa Barbara. Joey agreed. When Joey arrived in Santa Barbara there was Donna! She said she came with cold meat loaf sandwiches. It was only a matter of time before Joey, being the fashionista he was, started helping her with the different clothes, styles, and colors she would wear to photo shoots. In fact, she was the girl on the "wash that gray right out of your hair" commercials of the 60s and 70s.

One afternoon while they were taking their normal break, the inevitable finally happened. They had sex. Black coffee and smoking cigarettes, cold meat loaf sandwiches, and sex. Joey was in love with this woman and not only was she the girl of his dreams, she was the girl he wanted to marry. She parted ways with her producer boyfriend and moved up to the Bay Area with Joey. He was very supportive and understood because there were really no feelings there to begin with. Joey was just the opposite and shared so much in common with Donna that he gave her all the attention a woman could want.

Now happily living together in San Francisco, Donna continued her modeling career, mostly in Las Angeles, and Joey continued growing his house painting business. He now had a small crew to work with him. Joey was such a kind, cool guy to work for he had the same guys the entire time he owned the business. I can also say that when I worked with him painting apartments, he made it fun and enjoyable. He specialized in very tall ceilings that no one else wanted to touch and he bought the ladders that were needed to get the job done. He would charge large fees for the difficult places.

Joey and Donna were not only lovers but they were fantastic friends who enjoyed all the same things such as fashion, cold meatloaf sandwiches, red burgundy, black coffee, and sex as often as possible. Donna knew about Joey's past with men but it was the time of free sex and liberal thinking in California, so it didn't faze her in the least.

Donna had a big photoshoot down in Los Angeles and she was going to fly down for a few days and fly back. Joey was not able to attend with her because he had to stay with the job as he worked right along with his crew on all the jobs. He believed if the owner was not present the job wouldn't get done correctly. He said to Donna, "Hey, the weather is beautiful - why don't you drive down with the top down in the Cadillac to L.A?" He said, "This way you will have a car to go see all your friends and get around without having to rent a car." Donna thought that sounded like a great idea so off she went heading down the coast to southern California. Joey was expecting to hear from her when she arrived at her hotel, but there was never a call. After several hours of trying to track her down, he received "the" call. Donna had been killed in a horrific car accident on Hwy. 101.

He said his whole world turned upside down again, and he was so lost and was "bunking into himself" for the next five years. Just like after Sam died. He said it truly takes at least five years to get over any loss, be it death, breakup, or any major shift to one's life. I believe that was Joey's true love and I also believe that is why he never looked for that love with a man. He would only look to male relationships for sex after losing Donna.

He eventually sold the barber shop and began working full-time in the architectural painting field. He and his crew enjoyed all types of painting jobs. He was happy for a change and glad to be away from doing hair after 25 years. He said the best way to get over any type of loss is to just get busy.

He created a routine of painting and then showering and going out and often time to the tubs. He said it's terrible when you can't even be in a steam room without someone saying, "Joe, is that you?"

One night he was at the tubs and in the vapors when he met a new friend. The guy eventually asked Joey if he cared to leave the place and go over to his house where he would find himself more comfortable. Joey accepted the invitation and went to this guy's house high in the hills of San Francisco overlooking the city. He said it was gorgeous. He would find out the next day that he went home with Randy Shiltz, the author of *The Band Played On*. Joey said he didn't know who he was nor did he care; he was a nice guy and they both needed company.

Joey was still missing Donna and Sam and others that had come and gone from his life. I believe this was preparing Joey to be stronger though the journey of life, because his most difficult challenge still waited ahead of him.

CHAPTER 4

Joey's business was flourishing with several big contracts and even some for municipalities around the Bay Area. He pretty much left hair behind and was doing all types of painting projects. He ended up working with Frank Lloyd Wright's grandson on a series of interiors for restaurants. With Donna gone and his life completely free, he stayed in touch with his friend John who was the one who had introduced Joey into the Bahai faith and a few other close friends including Peter Wilton who would later move to San Diego and open an antique store.

Joey and his crew were doing all types of painting jobs and he was so happy to be out of the hair business completely. He said he had a good run with it but it was time to be creative and add beauty in another way to the world. He believed in having a routine. Joey was big on two things. Making lists and having a set routine. It was one thing he taught me when I worked with him: there is a time for everything.

He would tell me many stories of how he would work out at the gym with Jack La Lane and how important it was to exercise. He believed in lifting weights and keeping a good body. He was short but muscular. In fact, Joey had several things that he would always break out and show me. One of them was this old photo album he had. Inside this album were invitations to all types of events from his famous clients. Napkins with notes and phone numbers and address they left for him when he worked at the Beverly Hilton.

He also had an old black and white photo of him posing naked with a few muscle heads from the gym. Not sure if that was popular in the 60s to pose naked after a workout, but to these gentlemen it looked like it was a proud moment for sure. Joey would always laugh and say, "Here is me and Jack Lalane and the guys posing naked." He had black and white pictures with signatures and business cards from the various studio executives and their wives. Joey was always rubbing elbows with many famous people of that era, but half the time he had no clue, because those things really didn't matter to him. Making woman look beautiful and glamourous was one of his favorite things.

He became attracted to house painting because he could take properties and restore them back to their natural beauty. He always believed in making something look just a little bit better than how he found it.

Joey's daily routine began with a workout that included lifting weights and jogging, a healthy balanced breakfast, and then meeting his crews and organizing the painting jobs for the day. Joey loved to carry one of those fake leather folders that had a yellow legal pad in it. This is where he kept all his lists and to-do's. Right up until his last days here on this planet, if you were picking him up, he would be in a pair of jeans and a navy-blue blazer with his fake leather folder under his arm. He was never without it and always ready to take a note at a moment's notice.

Even though he always claimed to not be into the Hollywood glitz and glamor, he still remained friendly with so many of his celebrity clientele from when he was cutting hair. He was still very popular within those circles and several women would want Joey on their arm as her escort for various events. Joey had that classic white hair and classic movie star look. He would have to tell many people his calendar was booked.

He also liked his personal time of going to the tubs and swimming, steam baths, and being the "queen of the vapors." He would make sure that even his time at the tubs was a scheduled and planned event. It was a way for him to unwind in many different ways. He also said going to the tubs was never something you did when you were having a bad day or didn't feel good about yourself. He always believed when you presented yourself you should strut like a peacock and that he certainly did.

Joey was keeping his life simple. He believed in having no debt whatsoever. He always said, "Jim, whatever you do, keep your expenses low because when the day comes that you don't want to get out of bed you won't have to. He said he never understood people who created all that debt and spent hours of their life ahead of time because they were going to have to pay it all back with the sweat off their own back. He was practical and not a material person and really prized any positions he had. He was happy he had sold the houses and was only worrying about a small rent. He sublet the barber shop to another guy so he kept the "tree house" apartment above the shop while he owned his painting business. He rented storage units where he stored all the ladders and equipment he needed for his painting jobs.

Years had passed since Donna and Sam had died, and he was feeling good both physically and mentally at this time. One beautiful spring day Joey decided to take a jog through Golden Gate Park before going to lift some weights. He was really enjoying the weather and sun that afternoon as San Francisco is more often on the chilly side. As Joey was running, he started to feel short of breath and began having a pain come across his chest like he had never felt before.

Having been in good physical shape, Joey hadn't really seen a doctor in years. He was a person that ate healthy, believed in monitoring the scale, and worked out on a daily basis. As he stopped running and began gasping for air and holding his chest, he began to approach people for help. He said he couldn't believe it but everyone he approached moved away from him and quickly walked off. He couldn't comprehend what was happening to himself physically, nor on a humanitarian level. He was astonished at the lack of compassion and that no one stopped to help.

He was able to make it to a phone booth in the park where he called 911 and then collapsed in the phone booth. The next thing he knew, he was in a hospital with doctors and nurses around him. He couldn't believe it. He was just in shock at how his body at 59 years old was having these issues. He hadn't realized at this point that he had suffered his first heart attack.

Joey said he was in a state of shock when they told him he had a heart attack. It just would not register in his mind. All he kept thinking was how he worked out, exercised, took vitamins, ate healthy, and avoided red meat and junk foods.

After running the usual barrage of tests, they put him on pills. It upset him that he was going to have to take heart pills the rest of his life. This would be a major resentment that he would carry with him until his last days. He would say, "Taking pills! Really? Is this what it has come to? What a bore!"

When he was released from the hospital, he was given his follow-up appointment with a cardiologist. Joey had no understanding, medically, of most of what they were telling him. As I have mentioned before, Joey had a certain naivety about him as many other people had guided him in the past though anything that was difficult to understand. This time all he would have is Bella and she was down in Florida raising the boys and running a busy salon.

When Joey went to his appointment, he was expecting the doctor to tell him that he would need some type of surgery to repair the damage that was done to his heart. The cardiologist would instead explain to Joey that he had a genetic disorder that he inherited from his father. That was just what Joey needed to hear - that he had inherited a bad heart from the man who had abused him his entire childhood.

He went on to explain that the heart could not be repaired, and that Joey was going to need a new heart. This made no sense to him at all. A new heart? Where am I supposed to get one of those? The doctor explained the waiting list process for a new heart transplant. He explained to Joey that all the exercising and taking good care of his body was paying off because he would have already been dead had he not exercised the way he had throughout his life. He told Joey he was a good candidate because of what good shape his body was in.

Joey was put on a transplant list and was given several options within the UC system of California. One was UCSD in San Diego where his friend Peter Wilton had relocated about a year earlier.

Once he was healthy enough again, he flew to Ft. Myers to his mother's. She had a cute apartment in an elderly complex in Ft. Myers. Bella had gotten her all set up. She, Derrick, and the kids were sure that all her pills were counted and that she had food, and she made it to all her doctor appointments. Mom was in her ninety's and still making her Italian sauce and delicious homemade pasta fagioli. Bella, always the caregiver, made sure everyone was doing well.

Joey loved his mother and always wished she would have left with him and David in 1955 to move to California. He enjoyed visiting her but would tell Bella that she was becoming an old woman and why this and why that. Joey was hard on his mother about aging. Joey didn't want to age and he certainly didn't want her to become "old." Bella was selling a condo she had there in Ft. Myers so while he was there, Joey helped out by painting it for her.

He also discovered a beach in Ft. Myers called Bunches Beach. True to his Taurus nature, he also figured out it was a gay beach where he could meet a trick or two and go back to their place. Joey loved the beach and he loved to be tan. Being Italian, he had great olive-colored skin that tanned easily.

Although Joey was sick and needed a heart transplant, it certainly did not stop him from living to the fullest in all areas of his life. After spending time in Ft. Myers, it was time to head back to the Bay Area to follow up with his doctor. He started to sell his equipment from his painting business and let the guys that worked for him know what was going to happen. A couple of them bought the business and let Joey work for them until he was ready to move to San Diego.

He began getting rid of a lot of stuff because he knew whatever he took to San Diego was going to have to be put in storage. His longtime friend Peter Wilton had a couple of empty garages at the antique store where he told Joey he could store his stuff while he was going through the surgery.

Joe sold everything and was working here and there. He would have a couple more heart attacks before realizing he could no longer paint and was going to have to pack it in once and for all and head to San Diego. He let his friend Peter know that he would be heading south ASAP. He hated leaving the Bay Area and he would complain and compare San Diego to San Francisco the entire time I knew him.

CHAPTER 5

There is not a doubt in mind that as I sit to write this chapter, Joey is with me as I write. When I was writing the preface, I received those two calls from Poughkeepsie NY. Now tonight it is very late as we approach the magical day of 11/11. A portal where I write my goals and watch with amazement as the year passes, that most everything that is written on the list is manifested. I go to YouTube music and the second song I hear is Bill Withers' "Lovely Day." This was one of Joey's and his sister Bella's favorite songs, and he would sing very loudly when the chorus came on. He loved to celebrate a lovely day! The joy I feel as I write this chapter, knowing that it is definitely going to be a lovely day!

Joey received a call one day from Peter in San Diego. Peter had just relocated to San Diego about a year or so earlier and opened his antique store. Joey was telling him how there is something wrong with his heart and he needed a new one. Joey, in his own simplistic naïve way, could not understand after all his years of taking care of himself and lifting weights and exercising, how he could need a new heart. It simply made no sense to him.

He really thought that this kind of stuff only happened to obese people. As we know, Joey never really understood people who allowed themselves to get into a situation where they were overweight. No doubt about it, Joey was what they would call now a "Fat Shamer." Certain things just made no sense to him. He really saw overeating as gluttony, and would say things like, "They just need to learn to back away from the table." Or something like, "Oh isn't that a shame he didn't know enough to stop eating."

During this conversation Peter mentioned that Joey should come to San Diego because of UCSD Hospital and the great medical care that was available in San Diego. After several calls back and forth, Joey decided it would be time for him to wrap up the painting business and move to San Diego. This was where he was being led to by Baha'u'llah. Joey always said when Baha'u'llah wants you in a certain place you will end up there.

Peter of course delighted in helping Joey get rid of a lot of his stuff. He knew Joey needed money and was more than happy to seize on the opportunity to sell some of

Joey's antiques he had acquired over the years in the Bay Area. There was never a moment like a vulture swarming in the sky over dead road kill that Peter would not seize an opportunity to make a buck at someone else's expense.

Joey would often joke about all the old ladies Peter would make friends with. Joey would say, "Look, he pals around with them just waiting for the day they will die so he can liquidate their estate and sell all their antiques." As usual, Joey was pretty much spot on. Most of the old ladies Peter knew had come into the shop browsing antiques so he had already sized up their tastes and inventory of antiques before befriending them.

Joey would become so irritated because he was the one that got Peter into interior design and window design by getting him a job up in the Bay Area. He also introduced Peter to many of his friends. In fact, he would later tell a story of how he introduced him to some friends up in the Bay Area. Peter apparently borrowed money from one of them so he could move to San Diego, and then he never paid the guy back. The guy passed away and Joey was upset he never offered to give the money back. The sad part for Joey was that he would start to figure most of this out about Peter after arriving in San Diego.

He said he couldn't believe how this guy turned out to be such a phony. He forgot Joey knew where he came from. He would say, "He wants to tell everyone his mother and aunt were the queen of England when I know he comes from a tumbleweed town in Texas."

Joey arrived in San Diego at Peter's apartment. Peter was very busy with the antique business. He rented a store on University Avenue and his apartment was directly behind the shop. It was an ideal situation for Peter. Joey was under the unfortunate assumption that Peter was wanting to help him when he kept telling him to come to San Diego. Peter was extremely selfish and didn't realize what taking on the responsibility of a very sick friend meant, or what it would require. For many years I was angry and never understood how someone could be so selfish. I have now matured spiritually to understand that it wasn't that Peter wouldn't, it was that he couldn't. He simply did not have the ability to be compassionate and loving unless it involved something that benefitted himself. A true opportunist.

It was only a short time after Joey arrived in San Diego that I would have the wonderful experience of walking into the antique store and seeing Joey sitting behind Peter's desk. He was very neatly dressed, snow white hair without a hair out of place, a smile, and twinkle in his eyes. I would have never realized how very sick he was at the time and how close to death he was. As each day passed, the muscle of his heart was failing. Not a valve, not a blockage, nothing that could be replaced except needing an entire new engine, as he would say.

Peter came over and introduced Joey as his dear friend from the Bay Area that had come to San Diego for a heart transplant. I remember thinking to myself that I didn't even know that they did heart transplants. I left off where they had put a baboon's heart in someone. I only knew of kidney transplants and liver transplants but in no way could I even fathom they could transplant a heart from one human to another.

After a nice conversation, Peter would tell me to stop by a little later after they closed the shop and we could visit at his apartment. I went home, grabbed some dinner and a shower, and went back to hang out with Jack and Joey. I walked in and Joey and I seemed to continue with the same wonderful connection we had earlier at the shop. We continued laughing and chatting, and it was as if I had known him my whole life.

Looking back at that initial meeting, I can see that Peter noticed our connection and appeared to be jealous. This pattern of Peter being jealous would continue until the end. Joey pulled out a joint and lit it up. He said, "Care to join me?" I indulged and we chatted and laughed. I was thinking about how this guy was waiting on a heart but you would never know it. What is he doing smoking a joint? I thought, "Well, what the hell at this point? Right?" The connection and feelings I had upon meeting him were as if we had always known each other.

I had stopped by the shop a few times after this meeting and this is when I could really see Peter's true colors coming out. There was another older man named Maurey who would come around and help Peter in the store. So Maurey, Joey, and myself were standing around laughing and enjoying our chat. There were no customers in the store at the time and Peter stormed over and said, "Hey guys, this looks bad for business. It's like an old queen sewing circle." It was with that that I politely excused myself and left. I told Joey I was sure we would see each other again.

CHAPTER 6

It had been a couple weeks since I had gone back to the shop to see Peter or Joey. After being insulted, I was not in a hurry to see Peter as I was beginning to see what type of person he was. My gut instinct has always been good when it comes to detecting a creep. The problem with me is, I usually stick around giving the person the benefit of the doubt.

Joey didn't have it easy living with Peter. After three days they say, company is like fish - it stinks. Well Peter didn't hide his continued annoyance that Joey was there. Joey was not a regular house guest. They had been friends for over 30 years and Joey was a very sick man in need of a heart and as each day passed, he was closer and closer to his end. That didn't seem to matter to Peter and he really didn't seem to be able to grasp the seriousness of the situation. Even if he could grasp it, he was so self-centered that it most likely would not have mattered.

Peter had this great big white cat he named Spook. Cute name for an albino cat. The cat took to Joey and you could sense Joey had such a gently way about him that animals instinctually gravitated towards his kindness.

Peter was making it more and more obvious that Joey was cramping his lifestyle. He actually came right out and said it. In fact, one-night Peter decided to have a "trick over" and told Joey to make himself scarce as he had a young man coming over. Knowing him, it was most likely a paid escort. Peter often said having a wad of money in his pocket made him horny. In any case, I remember Joey telling me the story some years later and how insulted he was.

Joey would get so angry because he was the one who took Peter under his wing in the early years and got him a job in interior design and window decorating and store displays. He remembered where Peter came from. I remember one night Peter invited me over to have some dinner and hang out with him and Joey. It was a nice candlelight dinner with great background Diana Krall jazz music playing in the background. It had lots of ambiance for sure. Peter was definitely one that liked to create an atmosphere, at least for appearances. Peter's apartment of course was decorated with very nice pieces and the artwork on the walls were lit perfectly as if they were in a museum. Each piece with its own soft, thin light above it. He would often have some long story about where the artwork came from and later Joey and I would crack up as Joey would say, "Did you hear that crap about that painting?" He said Peter acted like he knew Picasso and that he was around when the Mona Lisa was painted. He would also ask me, "What's wrong with this guy? He thinks I am going to buy his crap about his mother being the queen of England. Not when I know where he was raised in Texas." Joey was so real and transparent, and the last thing he was into was a phony baloney, as he would say.

The dinner that evening was nice. Joey and I would go on talking with great laughter, and we were developing great rapport. One could see Peter was becoming quite perturbated to say the least. We all sat around in this very formal living room when Joey asked, "Care to smoke a joint?" He pulled out a perfectly rolled joint and a Bic lighter ready to go. I was shocked I guess because here was this guy waiting for a heart transplant playing Puff the magic dragon. I remember thinking at the time if I was in his situation, I would most likely be doing the same thing. Well, I have never been one to pass up a good time or a nice joint, so I participated and the laughter and the conversation was as if we had been old friends forever.

Joey was the type of person you met and had an instant connection with. Joey loved a good joint and a good conversation. He was telling stories of his barbershop in San Francisco after he gave up doing women's hair at the Beverly Hilton being "Mr. Joseph." He would often boast about how he could do an updo and a color and never get a drop on the tuxedo he was required to wear. He loved to tell stories about his old days doing hair and his adventures as he rubbed elbows with some of the Hollywood elite of the day. None of it really impressed him then and I supposed that was just another special quality of his. When he told his stories, it was without pretention or any type of bragging. He simply had a great time and loved to share his stories with the amazement he experienced as each thing happened in his life.

I am really more amazed looking back on that night more than ever before, as I realize just how very ill my newfound friend was. His heart was failing at a rapid pace and you would have never known it sitting there laughing with him. The dimples and the smile, the white hair, and a guy who could make jeans and a t-shirt look like a million bucks. He never once acted sick or really spoke about why he was in San Diego waiting for the heart.

The night was getting on and it was obvious that Peter had other plans as he was trying to wrap up this part of his evening. The one thing about Peter, at least with me as an empath, was that he was as readable as the *New York Times*. He defiantly wore his feelings on his face. I am sure there was another trick waiting in the shadows for Peter to be done with his entertaining and his dinner plans. We all said good night and again the connection I had with Joey was just the oddest thing. I bid him farewell and assured him we would see each other again for sure.

The next time I saw Joey was when Peter had an open house at the antique store. My ex-partner Jeff, who had introduced me to Peter when I was looking for 1920s décor for my new apartment after separating from my wife, was unemployed and had some cooking talents. Peter wanted to help Jeff out so he hired him to do the catering for this open house at the antique store. While Peter and Jeff were entertaining guests, Joey and I had more time to hang out and chat. It didn't take long to realize his quick wit and his ability not to miss a thing. Joey would point out things Peter was saying about the antiques he was trying to sell. Of course, Peter had a story for every piece he sold. Most of the stories were not true though. Most of the items were acquired from old ladies he worked on prior to their departures, or he would find items at the San Diego Swap Meet and just create an amazing backstory about the item.

This would be the visit where Joey gave Jeff the name that he would call him for the rest of our days. When people would enter the open house Jeff would greet them and say, "Won't you try the Radicchio? It's stuffed with goat cheese!" From that moment on Jeff would be referred to as "Radicchio." Joey was also an empath and never cared for Chris as he saw right through him.

I think it is also worth noting that the sound of Jeff's voice was very high pitched and feminine with a Rhode Island accent. This would of course only egg Joey's boyish type side to come out and giggle and repeat, "Won't you try the Radicchio?" over and over. Despite the pain and learning experiences I had because of my relationship with Jeff, Joey and I enjoyed countless laughs over the years just by saying, "Try the Radicchio; it's stuffed with goat cheese!"

I would visit Joey a couple more times and see him as he was waiting for the heart. On one visit we were talking about what was required for a heart transplant to have a match. He continued on with the list of so many things that had to match such as blood type, BMI (which is your height and weight), your rib cage size, and many other things that would be required. Not only are hearts difficult to come by, as all organs are, but also you have to worry about all the different things that have to be in perfect order for you to have a perfect match. I really marvel when I look back at the situation because Joey was days away from being called to his maker and you would never have known it. It reminds me of the Billy

Crystal bit when Billy does an imitation of Fernando Llamas on the Johnny Carson show and said, "It's not how you feel, Johnny, it's how you look." Joey was the epitome of that statement, and for the most part always looked good, with a great beaming smile, dimples, and a sparkle in the eyes that could only be that of an angel sent to earth. His humor could be silly and that of a teenage mischievous boy. Encourageable for sure!

After a couple of weeks had passed without hearing from Peter, I called the shop to say hello and ask how Joey was doing. When Peter answered the phone, he sounded very rushed and had his "I'm important voice" on. I said, "Hey Peter, how is it going?" He said, "I'm really busy right now can we talk later?" I said, "Sure, but I was calling to see how Joey is doing." He said, "Oh, he is in the hospital. He is over at UCSD waiting for his heart." I was shocked and asked Peter if he had been over to the hospital. His response was, "Hey honey, I'm trying to run a business here! I don't have time to play nursemaid to Romain." I was once again learning just how selfish and self-centered some people can be. After recovering from my complete disgust from his attitude, I simply asked him what Joey likes. Since we just met only a few weeks ago, I had no idea what one brings to a dying man in the hospital. He said, "Oh honey, he's an old hair dresser who worked at the Beverly Hilton. He still loves to keep track of Hollywood and the stars. Bring him some of the rags like *People* or the *National Enquirer.*" He told me no matter how sick Joey was, he would eat that stuff up.

Off to the nearest Ralphs I went! I indeed bought *People* magazine and the *Star* and the *Enquirer*. I kept thinking, "Is this silly what am I doing? I am going to visit a man who will most likely be dead in a week. I just met this guy and have no idea why I am doing this, other than the fact that his friend is a selfish jerk." Yet looking back, even then I seemed to have been called to the situation. I was being called to Joey. Little did I realize it was a higher calling that would lead me to many years of learning, love, and laughter.

Upon arriving at the hospital, rag mags in hand, they told me at the front desk he was in the CCU which was the ICU for heart patients. Luckily this was back in the days before HIPPA when people's privacy was not so well guarded. I couldn't help but wonder if this guy had a family, and if so, why were they not there at his dying bedside. It seemed like he only had Peter in his life.

I walked to the nurse's station and she showed me to his room. He was directly across from the nurse's station with big sliding glass doors. In the CCU all patients are on display, so to speak, and being very carefully monitored with constant beeps, bells, and ringing. How anyone was supposed to get rest I have no clue. The nurse told me to please keep the visit short to about 15 minutes as he was weak. I walked in, and he looked up and said, "Jimmy? What are you doing here?" I said with my very best fake chuckle, "Well I heard you couldn't come and visit me so I thought I would stop by. With all the things you are hooked up to, now wouldn't be a good time to ask you if you would care to share a joint." He smiled and said, "I wish." I said, "Hey, I heard you like these Hollywood trash mags, so I'll put them on the bed. He asked who told me he liked these rags, so I told him it was Peter and he smiled.

We carried on with small talk for a short while before my 15 minutes were up. I am sure glad I didn't know at the time how close to the end he was, or I think the visit would not have been as relaxed and natural. I asked him if he had any family and he said his sister Bella was closing up her shop down in Naples Florida and was coming in the next day to be with him. I remember thinking, "Oh thank you God, he is not dependent on the old miserable queen who was more interested in selling dead peoples' belongings than taking care of a friend."

After he told me about his sister coming, we were just chatting and I was doing my best to wrap things up. I remember not wanting the conversation to end though. It was then, at that moment that I asked him one simple question. The answer he gave me would change my life forever.

The question that came out of my mouth, like it was someone else speaking the words was: "Joey would you mind if I asked you a personal question?" He said, "No, what?" I asked, "Do you pray?" He repeated, "Do I pray?" He then began to giggle and laugh as only he could, monitors going off and the nurse coming in to tell me I had to go and we need not to get Joe excited! After the nurse left, he said, "What do you think someone would do when they are waiting on a heart?" I said, "True, silly question."

He said yes, he prayed but not to who you'd think he would pray to. I said, "I figured since you were Italian American that you were raised Catholic." Little did I know he was only half Italian. In any case he said, "I pray to Baha'u'llah." I said, "Who?" He repeated, "Baha'u'llah. I am Bahai and have been ever since I came to California in the 1950s. My friend Bob got me into the Bahi faith when he took me to my first fireside chat." To be honest, I wasn't buying into it, only accepting that this was his story, and I had the opinion of to each their own and that is personal to the person. Who am I to judge at a time like this? This man is clinging to what he believes will bring him a heart and keep him alive.

I still to this day do not know what caused me to ask him that question. The only thing looking back that I can think that caused me to ask the question was that I had been exploring my own faith in a way I never had in the past. I had just been through an emotionally painful divorce so self-exploration was pretty much at the forefront of my life. I was very involved at this point in my life in a nondenominational church called The Science of Mind. It was started by Ernest Holmes in the 1920s. Earnest Holmes had studied under Mary Baker Eddy of the Christian Scientists. He left the Christian Science faith and started his own because unlike the Christian Scientist, Ernest Holmes believed that the Spirit works through doctors as well to heal us. I really enjoyed going to church in Mission Valley in San Diego. It was a service like I never experienced where I felt loved and accepted for the first time in my life. I was also being taught ironically in the Science of Mind faith that thoughts were things and you could believe until you manifested. This was starting to tie in with a book I read called the *Magic of Believe* by Claude Bristol. Now that I reflect on all of the steps along the journey of my faith, each step happened exactly as it should have at the exact moment it was supposed to happen. Having been raised Catholic, the Science of Mind Church with the wonderful Rev. Kathy was a place I didn't feel like I was going to hell for being a gay man.

Joey was so passionate when he spoke Baha'u'llah's name and when he said he was Bhai. Then he looked at me with those big brown sparkling eyes and said, "Please understand there is nothing I have ever asked Baha'u'llah for that he has not given me. I have asked him for a heart.

He has brought me all the way to San Diego, to a part of California that is not my home, for a reason. He never disappoints; my heart is coming, trust me it is coming. He sent me here for a reason." He said the worst that would happen is the heart wouldn't come and he would end up spending eternity with Baha'u'llah and all those he ever loved including his dog Taurus. He had a poodle named after his birth sign.

I thanked him for sharing that with me and I told him no matter who he prays to I am sure everything will turn out just fine. I knew when I said it, I really didn't believe at all that everything would be just fine. I told him to take care of himself and I would see him soon. He said, "Alwad u adha." I said, "What?" He repeated it, so I said it back: "Alwad u adha." Little did I know this is a Bahia greeting and goodbye and we would share it for the remainder of our friendship.

Once our visit was over and we said our goodbyes, I walked down the CCU hallway heading for the elevator with crocodile tears streaming down my face. Anyone who knows me knows how sensitive I am, so that was not unusual. I was thinking he was such a cool guy and really touched my life. I really wish I would have met him sooner in my life. I was saying to myself, "That poor bastard thinks some dude named Baha'u'llah is going to bring him a heart. I have a better chance of pigs flying out of my ass then he has of getting a heart." I pretty much figured I would take a back seat now and wait for the call from Peter telling me Joey had died. I was prepared for the call as I knew that it was only a matter of time. I was glad I didn't know Bella or any other family members at that time because I would just have to go through saying "I'm sorry" to people I had never met. Oh well, it was nice to know him for that short time. I had also thought this was a good time to start distancing myself from Peter. He was such a pompous ass, and I really wanted nothing to do with him any longer. He lacked the character and integrity that I still require in my close relationships. My thoughts were, "Nice knowing ya, Joey."

CHAPTER 7

7:00pm, November 3rd, Camp Pendleton, located just up the coast in Oceanside, California. During a training mission a young Marine is accidently shot. Friendly fire, man down, call 911. Life flight helicopter arrived on the training field to find a courageous young Marine fighting for his life. He simply signed up to do his duty to fight for his country and ended up a victim of friendly fire and now was fighting for his life. He was only 21 years old and would make his transition to the other side in flight on the way to UMC San Diego. His parents were contacted and they gave consent for the organ donation to begin.

November 4th my phone rang. It was the 90s so I let it roll to the answering machine to screen the call. It was Peter's voice, so I picked up. My first thought was that he was calling to tell me Joey was dead. He said in his annoying arrogant voice, "Hey honey, I thought you would like to know that Romain got his heart last night!" He asked me if I had made it up to the hospital to see him last night. I said, "Yes, around 6:30pm." He told me it must have been right after I left. They immediately started prepping him for surgery because they were able to take the heart warm and not have to ice it before giving it right to Joey. I remained in disbelief. I had goose bumps up my arms. In fact, there is seldom a time when I don't tell "the story" that I don't get goose bumps. It was the day I truly learned about faith, healing, and the power of belief. I had written my new friend off as dead and he knew the entire time that Baha'u'llah was bringing him a heart. There was never a doubt in his mind. You could see the belief in his twinkling eyes that HIS heart was coming.

There was never a doubt in Joey's mind that his faith and the power of belief would bring him the heart he so desired. He said he believed because he knew his work for Baha'u'llah was not done here yet. He had all three things required to manifest. He had desire, belief, and expectancy. He was expecting the heart he knew he would receive. His belief was unwavering. It reminds me of lyrics from an old Bob Dylan song from his *Saved* album. The song is called "Precious Angel": **Ya either got faith or ya got unbelief and there ain't neutral ground.** This is how Joey lived his life, he was never in the middle when it came to his faith or beliefs. He also had a stubborn streak and whatever he believed, he believed.

It was quite some time after the surgery that I would reconnect with Joey. I was doing my best to distance myself from Peter and any other toxic people I had acquired along the way. It seems at times that life has been a journey of slaying dragons in the labyrinth and ridding myself of people I no longer care to be around.

Bella arrived from Ft. Myers Florida the same day that Joey went in for his surgery. She was so close to her brother and was by his side for every minute. Keep in mind she had her own salon in Naples Florida and her family she had to leave to nurse Joey back to health. Bella is made of the same cloth as her brother and the love shined through more than ever during his time of need. She made many sacrifices to get to San Diego by closing her shop and as a self-employed person sacrificing the months of income that she lost as a result of being away from home. Bella had the same determination and belief her brother had, so she was not leaving San Diego until he was able to care for himself and live on his own.

Because Joey was from the Bay Area, the only people he really knew in San Diego were me and his self-centered friend. The "friend" who was more interested in harvesting old people's antiques for his own profit than he was in helping his friend of over 30 years. Joey had to go to a recovery house for transplants and other people's families from out of town who had family being operated on at the hospital. While Joey was in the hospital, Bella had asked Peter if she could stay at his place. He was so irritated she asked to stay at his place while he was in the hospital, that he said, "One night and anything more would cramp by style."

Bella and Joey had a cousin out in an area called La Mesa, which wasn't very far from San Diego. Bella stayed with her cousin on and off as hotels were costly, but she didn't have a car to get back and forth either. Because Joey and I were not close friends and I had never met Bella, she had no way of contacting me or even knowing I existed. She was stuck in a big way. Hindsight being 20/20, she could have stayed with me. I would have welcomed it as it was a lonely time in my life and she could have stayed at my bungalow that I was renting at the time in North Park.

Once he regained some strength, Joey was discharged from the main hospital and was transferred to the rehab house on the campus. Bella was also allowed to stay with him and take him to the various appointments he would have at cardiac rehab, occupational therapy, and various physical therapy. As if that wasn't enough to fill the days, he also had classes he would have to attend on how to take his anti-rejection medications which included over 40 pills a day! He would often say "taking all these pills is a big bore." He was a guy who worked out with Jack

Lalane and took great care of his health, so the idea of having to take medications for the rest of his life really bugged him, to say the least.

Bella and Joey moved into the rehab house. Bella was grateful to have a place to stay as she could no longer afford a hotel or a rental car, especially not knowing how long she would be in San Diego. It would only be a few nights after they were staying at the rehab house that Bella walked up to the store and bought groceries to stock the kitchen. She made friends with the other families staying at the rehab facility and soon began cooking their mom's famous Italian sauce with pasta. She also cooked lasagna and other dishes she knew she could feed many with. The other families were also going through various issues and were always more than happy to enjoy some of Bella's delicious cooking.

Bella again showed continuous support and love for Joey. He was not always the easiest patient because often times he didn't understand what was going on, and Bella was the one who had to care for him. Because she was nine years younger than him, not only was she caring for her older brother but she had their mom back in Ft. Myers who was in her late 80s that she was caring for. Their father lived up in Poughkeepsie with his second family that he created after Joey's mother finally divorced him. It wasn't until after years of destruction to her and the rest of the family that she finally chose to leave him, something Joey never really forgave his mother for.

Joey and Bella would spend weeks at the rehab house which was downhill from the hospital. Bella would push Joey in his wheelchair up the hill to the main hospital every day to be sure he made all his classes and appointments about living with his new heart. Although Joey was very light and didn't weigh much, for her to have to push him up that hill several times a day took a great deal of not only physical strength but love. This would go on for the better part of two months.

Once Joey was discharged from the rehab house, they literally had no place to go. Joey had no apartment; Peter was, as you may have figured by now, unavailable on many levels. The two headed to the only place they knew to go, which was their cousin out in La Mesa. Bella and Joey would stay there and go back and forth to San Diego for his appointments. Bella was getting to the point where she had to get back to Ft. Myers to her mother, her family, and her hair salon business that she had left behind. Their cousin said they would help Joey get all settled and get him to his doctor's appointments, but just like Peter, they tired of the caretaker role very quickly. Many people have no idea what it takes to take care of another person, especially from something as major as a transplant surgery.

Bella headed back to Ft. Myers and Joey, after just a few short months, could no longer get along with his cousin and had to move out. Despite how he felt physically, he called Peter to help him find an apartment in San Diego on a bus route that would get him back and forth to the hospital. You talk about determination! At this point Joey was out of his life savings. All the money he had earned off the sale of properties up in Mt. Claire and the money he made from the hair business and the painting business was gone. Because of his physical situation he was not in any shape to start cutting hair or painting again. He was dependent on the little of money he had left over and his social security disability.

CHAPTER 8

I had not seen Joey since the night he told me he was going to get the heart. I had not met Bella yet as I am not the type to enter into anyone's family during such an emotional time. Bella was back in Naples at the salon cutting hair and caring for her mother and family. Joey was determined to stay in San Diego as he idolized his cardiac surgeon. He would always brag about how young and smart and bright she was, and then go on to say, "You know, she is a lesbian too." He would always say it with pride that a lesbian did his heart transplant.

One day Peter called me out of the blue and said, "Hey, I am picking up Romain. Do you want to join us for dinner at Café 11 in Hillcrest?" He also told me that a female attorney friend would be coming along as well. Peter picked me up in his truck in North Park. I was living on Boundary Street at the time in a little back bungalow. This was my own little slice of peace and quiet as I was rebuilding my life after my divorce. I loved those craftsman cottages along the alleys and canyons of San Diego.

We started driving out El Cajon Blvd and we were heading East. We kept driving and driving and driving until I finally asked Peter, "Where the hell did you get him an apartment?" I think he said like 79th street or something way up in numbers. Back in the 1990s when you headed that far east it became poorer and poorer as the street numbers went up.

We finally arrived at Joey's. The apartment had the typical San Diego look. It was like an old 1950s motel two-level, and Joey lived in an apartment on the first floor. Peter was kind enough to think Joey could use some company so he lent Joey the use of his cat, Spook. Who lends their cat to someone? In any case, we picked Joey up and headed to Café 11. It was so great to see him and it was as if no time had passed. He just seemed a little frailer and a little puffy in the face from all the medications he was on for anti-rejection of the heart.

It was great to see him, and I was still in amazement that he manifested a heart just as he said he would. At dinner we were telling "the story" of how Joey manifested his heart by knowing Baha'u'llah would bring him the heart. The more we talked about the heart, the more annoyed Peter became. The old queen wore his feelings on his face. The dinner ended and we drove Joey home. Joey and I chatted all the way up the boulevard with Peter saying nothing except a few words here and there.

We dropped Joey off and then sat in the car in front of Joey's apartment. Peter lit a joint and he began to rant on and on about how embarrassed he was that all Joey did was talk about illness all night long. I tried to reason with him, but Peter, being himself, wasn't hearing it. We drove down the boulevard while he continued to bitch and moan all the way back to my house. I could not wait to get out of the truck. Jeesh! More and more obvious why Peter had no lover. Can you say Bitter table for one Bitter?

Over the next few months, I called Joey a couple of times to check on him. I was caught up at the time in my corporate life as a Marketing Manager for a mail order company and didn't have much free time of my own. I called him once and he told me he was letting some kid stay with him who was helping him out with expenses. I really didn't like the sound of this. My instincts were correct. The guy beat Joey up for money. Joey had called the cops and had to have a restraining order put on the kid.

A few months later I called him and got a disconnected number recording. I had no choice but to call Peter and ask him how Joey was. He said, "Oh Romain always comes out smelling like a rose." He told me Joey was living in a small cottage on the corner of 35th street and El Cajon Blvd. He said it was the very last cottage and to just go knock on his door.

One Saturday morning I woke up and was feeling very lonely. I had this heavy empty feeling that I had no friends at all. My life had changed so much over a short period of time. All the friends I had when I was married pretty much just slipped away. Not to mention I had a lot of feelings of shame and humiliation about having gotten married and then divorced and coming out. That was a lot to take on all at the same time in anyone's life.

A while back, I fell madly in love with a gothic style iron framed bed I saw in the window of a store in Hillcrest. The price of the bed was $2800. That price was so far out of reach for me I decided to take a picture and see if I could get it made cheaper in Mexico, so I headed to Rosorito Beach south of Tijuana. The wonderful thing about living so close to Mexico back in those days was that you could cross the border and get furniture made or a custom upholstery job done for half the cost you could in San Diego. I had driven down months earlier with a picture of the bed and had it made for $800. It was going to be months before it would be ready, though. The crazy thing is, I still sleep in that bed today and brought it with me from San Diego to the East Coast.

One afternoon while in the area, I decided to drive over to 35th street to check on Joey. There were five cottages in a row to my left and his was the last cottage. They were all one-bedroom places and very small. These places were in pretty run-down shape and it looked like each cottage had multiple Mexican families living in them with way too many people in a small place. There was no grass, just concrete and trash and junk everywhere. There were mattresses all over the place and many other things that others had left behind. Joey was truly living in the ghetto.

I knocked on the door of the last cottage and Joey answered the door. He somehow didn't seem that surprised to see me. He said, "Oh Jim, I knew you would be coming. I got the message from above." He looked amazing with his glowing smile, nice clean white pressed t-shirt, and jeans without a hair out of place. There was the fresh smell of reefer permeating the place. I said to him, "Smells nice in here." He said, "You can smell that?" Joey had no sense of smell. I asked him where in the heck was he finding somebody to buy weed from. He said, "Oh that's easy; these young guys come by on bikes. They are so nice I trade them a haircut for a few joints."

He invited me in and we had a great time catching up, again. I said, "Do you want to head south and go to Mexico with me and have lunch? I have to pick up a bed I had made down in Rosorito." He said, "Give me a minute and I will be right with you." He grabbed a nicer shirt and of course his fake leather note pad and hopped in my truck. He brought some water and some cut-up apples and some joints for the ride.

We had the best day together laughing and getting to know each other and sharing all types of stories about faith, healing, and the power of belief. I took him to the Rosortio Beach Hotel. He was impressed because many of the stars during Bogie and Bacal's time hung there. We had a table overlooking the beach and enjoyed tacos and burritos and a margarita each.

We picked up the bed and headed back toward the US border. There was always such a long wait at the Tijuana border, but we had not a care in the world. We laughed about the dumbest things and shared stories about our lives. He told me about his experiences with Donna and Sam, the Beverly Hilton, and so many other fantastic stories. We both found out we shared the love of old music from Frank Sinatra, so I put on some Sinatra and we sang all the way back to San Diego.

The sun was setting when I pulled up to 35th Street to drop him off. It was such a wonderful day I didn't want it to end. He said, "Please don't let so much time go by before you come again and here is my new number. I'm up early; come by anytime."

CHAPTER 9

A few more weeks had gone by and I was busy traveling for the company I did the catalog marketing for. I was doing trade shows around the country so I was usually gone more than a week out of each month. My relationship with "Radicchio" as Joey called him, was becoming more and more toxic by the week. My self-esteem was at the worst it had been in my life since I was about 14 years old. I was feeling alone and defeated. I had lost my condo at the beach, been through a divorce, and gone through a marriage I should have never entered into. I was in a bad way.

I began stopping by the 35th street bungalow on the regular. I would come by in the late afternoon and Joey and I would usually start with a glass of Carlos Rossi Red Burgundy and then he would inevitably pull out a "ceremonial joint," because he said every day was a celebration. He would often start singing "It's a Lovely Day" by Bill Withers.

"When I wake up in the morning, love
And the sunlight hurts my eyes
And something without warning, love
Bears heavy on my mind

Then I look at you
And the world's alright with me
Just one look at you
And I know it's gonna be
A lovely day."

He would often sing this and smile as he was pouring the Carlos Rossi out of the big jug.

Those were some of the most delightful afternoons and evenings I ever spent with Joey. It was like I was entering a world filled with peace, love, laughter, and lessons. I never left without one lesson or another. Different seeds of wisdom my white-haired friend would share. His place was so small but everywhere you looked he had a piece of something he could share a story about.

He had a collection of large crystal door knobs which he said he and a few friends stole from Liberace's front door in Vegas. The paintings were nicely framed replicas of cafés in Paris. The small love seat and side chair were covered to match. When you scanned the book case there were some books that jumped out immediately.

The first one was his original copy of Napoleons Hills' *Think and Grow Rich*. I realized as we talked more and more that he was always teaching me about manifestation. He also had a book about the minds of serial killers. He was the gentlest man and at the same time would tell me how he was fascinated with the minds of those murderers and how could people be like that?

On his book shelf was his faux leather photo album with all his previous clients' notes and invitations to all the parties over the years. He was very proud to sit down and go over the album on occasion.

I would feel bad sometimes when I would go to see Joey because as I walked down the driveway towards his bungalow, I would pass the other units with their old mattress and overcrowded conditions. Their doors would often be wide open, Mexican music playing and kids running in and out. Then there was Joey all the way in the back in his own world as if none of that was going on at all.

One Saturday afternoon I stopped by and he was working out around the outside of his place and going back and forth into one of the garages that were at the end of the driveway. There were four garages which the landlord rented to various people for storage. He was telling me the landlord was letting him use one of the garages for his "stuff." Joey was a borderline hoarder, no questions there.

Joey said he told the landlord he would manage the place for him as the people moved out, that he would "doll the places up." He also told the landlord to start renting to working people and stop renting to people without references or employment. The landlord had agreed as he was almost 80 years old and owned many apartments all over 35th street that he wanted to sell because he was retiring and downsizing.

Each time I would visit there were be noticeable improvements coming down the driveway and each time a unit was empty he would be painting them "Arizona White." This is how Joey believed he would recover with his new heart. He acted as if it was a small operation and just went on living his life as he always did. When I would tell him maybe he shouldn't drink wine or smoke weed, he said they were natural and he had a 21-year-old heart that could handle it.

He said, "Hey kid, why don't you help me paint these places when they become available? You can come on the weekends and it will keep you out of trouble." I think he knew this was going to be his opportunity to plant more seeds. Always positive in nature and some sank in weeks, months, and are still sinking in today as I age.

We would spend hours on Saturdays and Sundays painting out the bungalows on 35th street. No more mattresses and trash cluttering the complex. All the front steps to each bungalow now matched, all painted in brick red. The bungalows were all painted peach with white shutters. He sectioned off the back so each bungalow had their own private yard. He eventually moved up closer so he was in the second bungalow as you entered the row.

Our time was spent listening to radio station with the Great American Song Book. Songs from Dean Martin, Sammy Davis Jr, Frank Sinatra, Rosemary Clooney, Ella Fitzgerald, and so many others. We would sing by the hour together and he was surprised that I knew the words. Especially the Sinatra tunes because I was a fan of Frank since I was really young, around five years old as I remember.

Within the year the places were painted and "all dolled up." Joey also helped me get through and end my toxic relationship with "Radicchio." We would usually finish up painting around 4pm and he would say, "Kid, it's about time we shut 'er down." We would clean our brushes and get everything ready for the next day before we would quit for the day. He would often finish during the week as I was at my corporate job.

One day after we "shut 'er down," he said, "I want you to watch this new show they have on in the afternoon." He said, "Come on in and we will relax with a little Carlos and a joint." The show was Jerry Springer. It was something I had never really seen until then. Joey would get such a laugh when they would all start beating on each other. Almost to the point of tears. His laughter was the reason I would laugh so hard. After a few episodes I told him it appeared fixed and he said no it was real. I never argued and often our afternoons were spent at the end of the day huddled in his back room where the TV was, watching Springer and filling the place up with smoke and laughter.

In one of our many conversations about life, love, and the pursuit of happiness, he said to me, "You don't really think much of yourself, do you?" I said, "What?" Wow, I was not expecting to hear that. I was quiet, he was quiet, and then without warning, my emotions became uncontrollable and I began to cry. He asked me what those tears were all about. I broke down and proceeded to tell him my insecurities and that I didn't feel attractive and that I would never ever find anyone. He looked at me with the most serious look and said, "I am so surprised because that is not what I see at all."

He said, "If I was younger, I would have asked you out because you are so smart and funny, not to mention that you have unique qualities you are not aware of." I said, "What unique qualities?" He said, "You are a healer and you were sent here to heal others." I laughed and said, "I am not doing that great of a job so far." He said, "How do you know? You have not contributed to my healing. Never underestimate yourself kid. I can see some gray hair coming through and just remember; the more gray you have, then people will begin to respect you more, and really start to listen to what you have to say. You have a message, kid, you just don't know it. Baha'u'llah has a plan for you. You just don't know it yet." After listening to all the wonderful things Joey was bringing to my attention, it was the first time in many years I felt good about myself! When I left that evening for my own small cottage, I was feeling better than I had in a long, long time. My takeaway was "I am enough just the way I am."

Anytime there were any vacancies in his complex, Joey and I would spend a day or so and paint it out with Arizona white and he would say, "Hey kid, you roll paint and I'll cut in. Then we would break for a small lunch and get back to work until 4pm. After that, it was time to shut 'er down for Carlos Rossi, a fat joint, and Springer. It was during these times that we spent together that he told me all the stories about Sam and Jenny, water skiing, his sister Bella, and his two wonderful nephews.

He bragged about his two nephews all the time. He would say, "You should see how handsome my nephews are." He said, "The older one takes after me! He has great muscles, is really built, and loves to work out." On one visit he showed me a tray that he had a silver coffee pot sitting on. It looked exactly like marble. He said, "You know, this isn't marble, my nephew painted this. He is a big artist at Disney and paints murals and does faux painting." He would say that one inherited his artistic talent and the other inherited his body and muscle.

Joey's landlord finally sold the bungalows of 35th street to another younger man. This guy was named John and he loved Joey. He would keep Joey busy with many projects. John would even buy the apartment complex next door, and Joey and I would maintain those places also.

One day I showed up at Joey's very upset. I had decided to walk out of my corporate job as I could no longer handle the owner of the company. The first place I went was over to Joey's. He said, "Kid, you never quit one job without another." I told him that I had started my own publishing company called Diverse Planet International Inc. and that I would be publishing newsletters for the gay community. It would be less than six months and the mailing I published for the first newsletter was to help people in the HIV community. I was very touched as my friend Tucker had died from HIV/AIDS complications just before they came out with protease inhibitors. It turned out I was ripped off when I bought the mailing lists. I was unaware that the lists had many deceased young men on it that had already passed from HIV/AIDS and their loved ones were calling my 800# raging angry. I felt horrible and like a loser.

I had financed the business on credit cards and just leased a new truck as well. I was in a financial crisis and don't think I could have gotten myself into a bigger mess. I was $25,000 in debt with the cards. Another $20,000 with the truck, with no money, no job, and very little money coming in. Life got real very quickly. I needed a job! In the meantime I collected unemployment and painted with Joey when he had work. I lived day-to-day buying a small bag of weed each week and drinking red wine, wondering what was I going to do.

Being the wise ole coot that he was, on one of our visits Joey began to give me his philosophy on debt. He said, "Kid, debt is so bad. I have no debt and not a worry in the world. When I had debt, there were reasons I had to get out of bed each day whether I wanted to or not. That's because I owed 'the man.'" He told me that if I live within my means, I will owe no one. "That is real freedom kid," he went on to say. "The less debt, the less you have to get out of bed." This sounded funny coming from a man who never stayed in bed until he had a heart transplant.

It was Halloween this particular year and I had asked Joey what he was going to be doing. He said certainly not giving candy and answering my door. He invited me over to have some dinner. He said he would cook his mom's lasagna with some pasta fagioli! I arrived at his place and it smelled wonderful. The atmosphere was magical with little white lights placed throughout, candles softly flickering with their flames dancing, and lots of ambience and mood lighting. In addition, Frank Sinatra singing "Witch Craft." Everything with Joey was choreographed perfectly.

I asked what the spicy autumn smell was. He said, "Oh, let me pour you a glass; it's my famous mulled wine. It's simmering on the stove." I looked in the pot and it was a mixture of cloves and cinnamon, with slices of lemons and oranges floating around on top. The base for "The Grog" as he called it, was none other than Carlos Rossi Burgundy.

He had the table set up in front of the front window of the bungalow. The blinds were closed with the music playing softly. The table was perfectly set up with these octagon black plates with matching black octagon bowels for salad and soup. Gold napkin rings with cloth napkins. It was so cool. I was sipping on my grog and we were chatting as he was taking the lasagna out of the oven.

We served ourselves and he had some wonderful San Francisco sourdough bread he bought at the bakery that day to go with the dinner and the pasta fagioli. This was one of those Joey evenings that remains as a wonderful moment in my life. As we were sitting there you could see the shadows of the kids coming to the door in their costumes. His focus was on me and the conversation. At one point I said to him, "Joey, the kids keep coming to the door." He said, "The light is off; can't they get the clue?" That means no candy, and he laughed. It was like he didn't miss a beat and he said, "Now what were you just talking about?"

I left having enjoyed the mulled wine and the wonderful evening. It was like I was caught someplace between reality and illusion. In fact, that would be the case throughout our friendship as I would enter into his world. Always leaving a little bit more fulfilled than when I arrived.

CHAPTER 10

I was starting to get a bit concerned as my unemployment was running out and I was not finding any jobs that I was qualified for. I was a high school graduate at the time, and had only risen up through the ranks because of my ability to use my skills to get me jobs.

I saw an ad in the classifieds of the paper for a social marketing director for the LGBTQ Center in San Diego. I asked Joey if he wanted to go with me for a ride to Los Angeles. He said he couldn't go because he was too busy. He asked why I was going to Los Angeles. I said, "Well believe it or not there is a place up there that sells manikin parts." He said, "What do you want with manikin parts?" I said, "Well I really want this job that I applied for at the LGBTQ center as Social Marketing Director and I am going to drop off a left arm with a note saying I would give my left arm to work as your Social Marketing Director."

I thought he would be happy for me but instead he was very negative and cynical about the whole thing. He said, "First off, why would you want a job working with 'The Gays?' And second of all, I would never drive up to Los Angeles to go work with a bunch of drag queens, cliques, and people whose elevator doesn't go to the top. You're forgetting, kid, I was in the hair business. I have never met one gay or lesbian without issues and I would never want to work in a place with all of them!"

I was crushed to say the least, and said, "Well we can disagree, but I am looking forward to getting it." He laughed and said, "It's your left arm, not mine."

I did get the job and learned a great deal over the seven years while I was there. We did campaigns to help get people tested for HIV, and to help find shelters for young, gay, homeless youth. I would be in denial if I didn't say that many of Joey's opinions were very true as it was very difficult to work in that environment. Be it my ego, stubborn pride, or whatever, I never would point out to him how he was right about my choice though. Nonetheless it's just another part of learning.

It was Memorial Day weekend and Joey and I decided we would just lay low because it was a holiday weekend in San Diego. We would just hang and do nothing all day.

I was cool with that and told him I would see him the following weekend. We talked almost daily on the phone, so I knew we would be in touch.

The internet was now in full swing and opened up a whole new world of communication. I was new to online chat and being just out of the toxic situation with Radicchio, I decided I would go online to see if I could find a trick. This was back in the day of AOL chat. I went to a chat room called AOL M4M chat. I met someone online. We talked and decided to meet. I then asked his age and he said he was 19 years old. I said, "No, I am 35 years old, so this will not work." After much banter, we decided to meet. I was beyond taken by this young man. I was so excited to share with Joey that I finally met someone who was nice!

I saw Joey the following weekend and was so excited to share the good news. I told him the story and he said, "Kid, you don't want a 19-year-old as your boyfriend." I said, "Why not? Are you jealous?" He said, "Hardly! Do you realize the work you are getting yourself into by getting involved with someone so young? Someone that young will be watching you and mimicking your every move. So that means you cannot be dragging this kid though the gay bars and bathhouses. He will need an education and go through many growing pains. If you do decide to take this kid on, remember you need to be a good example for him. You need to be both a boyfriend and a mentor, so do not take the responsibility lightly."

My new boyfriend also got a job working in the accounting office of the LGBTQ Center. Unfortunately, he shared with me the allocation of the grant funds that was going on and where my grant money was actually going and why my salary continued to be reduced. It was sad to realize that some of what Joey had warned me about was now happening to me. I utilized the situation to my advantage and decided to tell them I would only work 20 hours a week and that I had chosen to pursue a career in the medical field. They would need to work around my hours.

They agreed and for 18 months I went to college to get an Associate's Degree in Respiratory Therapy. Joey was so proud of me and said, "I want to go to your graduation." He also said, "Kid, your partner is watching and it won't be long before he also wants to go to college and do great things." I would say he is right because me and my soul mate have been together 22 years, and he has completed his Masters of Science degree in Computer Science.

I completed my Associates degree and Joey was so proud to be sitting in the front row with his faux leather legal pad folder in his navy-blue blazer and a pair of jeans and nice wing-tipped shoes. He and my partner were the only two that could attend as my family was all on the East Coast at the time.

Joey and I continued to paint together. He said to me one day, "We may have a big job coming up someday soon, kid." "Oh yeah, what is it?" I asked. He said, "You know there is a young guy who lives across the street in that house and I have been working with the police. I am seeing drug activity going on over there and I am concerned. There are all types of prostitutes and druggies coming and going at all times of the day and night. I have been taking pictures of the license plates as they come and go. I have been working with detectives and have also been in touch with the owner of the house. She wants me to help her fix it up after she evicts this guy."

Several weeks later the bust happened. Joey called it "Christian's House." He said he would pay me by the truck load to remove all the debris and help him fix the house up and get it ready for sale. I cannot begin to tell you how gross this place was! The guy was a meth head and never threw out his garbage. The entire yard and all the rooms were knee deep in trash. We used snow shovels to shovel the debris and take dump loads all day on the weekends to the dump.

One day we were listening to the old tunes and I thought of a book I read a few years before Joey and I met. It was called the *Way of the Secret Warrior* by Dan Millman. The oddest thing stuck me; it was like déjà vu. I remember when I was reading that book, I had a feeling I would also someday meet my own "Socrates." Socrates in the Dan Millman book was the mentor/angel that he had met when he was in college and taught him his most valuable life lessons.

As we were busy working, I decided to share the thought with Joey. I told him about the book and as I was explaining it to him, I said that this kid had met this "old man" and he taught the kid a great many things about life. It is sort of like you have taught me. I told him the odder part was that it was like I knew I would someday write a book about him and our friendship. He got quiet for a minute and them became very insulted. He said, "I just want you to know I am NOT an old man and I do not appreciate you calling me old!" I really didn't know that some people, especially older gay men, do not like to think of themselves as aging. I always equate being a young gay man to being a model. When you turn 30, you turn your card in because you are old and there is a new generation right behind you.

Well, the more I tried to explain the worse it seemed to get. We both got quiet. I continued to roll paint and he continued to cut in. We were not singing together with the tunes any longer as we usually would be doing. He was humming a bit. I wasn't sure how this was going to go and then he said, "Come on kid, it's about that time to shut 'er down and go relax with a joint and some

Springer." I smiled and we starting washing out the brushes and buckets so we could head across the street to Joey's bungalow. It was like walking into a time machine.

We ended our day smoking and watching Springer and laughing at the crazy people attacking each other for cheating on each other. He would say if they would only realize what they were doing to themselves. He said, "She could never find anyone like him again." Like him, he said? "Who would want a liar and a cheater, but that is all that poor girl thinks she is worth? Doesn't she know men are like busses - all you have to do is wait on the corner and another one will come." He would often try to reason out their behavior as we sat and watched. He did believe this stuff was real.

My 18 months in the respiratory program would pass quickly. I was working at many local hospitals for my clinicals. I wanted to work at Balboa Naval Hospital and had good opportunities to go work there. I worked part-time with Joey and the LGBTQ center and went to school full-time.

We finished the house across the street and it sold quickly. Joey was so proud that he was helping keep 35th street clean. I asked him what he planned to do now what we were done with this project. He said, "Kid, tonight I am going to be queen of the vapors and I am going to the Mustang!" The Mustang was a gay bathhouse on

University Ave near Florida Street. Ironically Joey didn't know that it used to be a Jack Lalane Health Spa when they were a chain before they went out of business.

"I am glad it's now the tubs instead of a gym," he said with a laugh. He also added, "Remember your comment about me being the old man you wanted to write about? Well kid, I am hot and I still got it. When I go to the Mustang all I do is put on a cowboy hat and a pair of mirrored sunglasses and my white towel with my nice Italian tan and I have to chase them away." That image is still burned into my mind and I get so silly just thinking about it. It's not how you feel, it's how you look.

I told him the last time I went to the tubs was on New Year's Eve the previous year. I told him I walked in and was handed a towel and a key to a locker. They also gave me a free calculator as a holiday gift that said "Club San Diego" on it. They had a free buffet going on and they were carving fresh hot pork with all the sides. I was ready to throw up thinking, "Who comes to a bathhouse to eat?" Somehow steam rooms, men running around in towels, and the smell of hot pork just seemed like something out of the movie *Bird Cage* or *La Cage aux Folles*. If Bette Midler was the entertainment I may have stayed.

I had never felt so lonely and awful at the tubs ever in my life. I walked in, went up to the locker, and decided this is no way to start a new year and walked right back out. The guy at the checkout said, "Leaving so soon? That was fast." Joey said, "First off kid, you never go to the tubs on any holiday weekends or during those peak times. Especially gay pride, stay away. Most importantly you are only supposed to go to the tubs when you are feeling your best. Your highest self-esteem. This is when you can strut yourself like a peacock and be noticed. You do not go there to raise your self-esteem. You must go when you believe you're hot and so will everybody else." Another valuable lesson from the queen of the vapors.

CHAPTER 11

September 11, 2001 changed everything. I remember going over to see Joey that day and he was, as usual, puttering around between the small bungalows on 35th street. He had his weight bench set up outside of the side door to his place so he could do some bench presses with light weights. He had his radio on the bench of course playing his America's Songbook. He had two garages filled to the top with "good stuff." He was a pack rat who loved garage sales. He loved having garage sales and reselling the stuff he bought at other garage sales.

When he was going in and out of the garages, I asked him what was in the garage on the end? He said "Oh, didn't I tell you? Peter is renting the garage for the overflow of his antique inventory." I was surprised and he said, "Hey kid, money is money. He rents the space; I chat with him and listen to his phony bullshit stories and he goes on his way."

I asked him if he was upset about what had happened to the WTC Towers in New York. He said, "Of course, but I'm not surprised as Baha'u'llah predicted great wars, fires, and floods." He quickly disappeared inside his house and came back out with a copy of the Bahai World News Service. He pointed to an article about the destruction that is coming and has been predicted. "You know kid, you outta really consider joining the faith and getting your Bahai card." I told him, "I do not do organized religion. The Catholics were the last one that had their chance with me. Now it's between me and my Christ within to improve." He agreed and then said, "But you still really should get your card. I'll take you to a fireside if you want." A fireside is the way that people in the faith gather in their homes with other members of the faith.

As I was looking at the stacks of boxes and junk piled to the ceiling in both garages, I felt anxious. I am very anti-clutter and anti-stuff: the complete opposite of Joey. He loved his stuff. I looked at this one box and it was written in black marker in big letters JIMS MOVIES. I said, "Hey, what is in that box with my name on it?" He started to giggle and said, "Those are a bunch of dirty VCR tapes and if anyone ever found them or anything happened to me, I wanted them to know they weren't mine." I said, "So you put my name on it?" And we both laughed.

I never felt very far from family or home for the 20 years I lived in San Diego. On 9/11, after they closed all air travel for a brief period of time, I had this awful feeling of how very far I was from my family in Connecticut. I decided that it was time to go home and see my grandmother who was 92 years old, as I knew she wouldn't be with us much longer. I had avoided home for the past five years as my mother was with a disgusting alcoholic and always created a scene. It was now time and I wanted to see family again.

Christmas would come that year and I told Joey I was taking my partner home to meet my family. He said, "Wow kid, this must be really long-term if you are taking him to meet the family." I said, "Joey, I know he and I have 15 years between us in age, but for whatever reason, it just works." Joey began to slowly accept that this was a steady thing at this point. He would always shake his head and say, "Kid I give you credit; you have a lot of work ahead of you." We flew back to Connecticut and I was able to see my mom and grandmother. Grandma was frail and old and she whispered to me, "Why is your mother still with that drunken fool?" I told her, "I know Meme, but what can you do?" She said, "I feel so sorry for her. She needs to get those knees fixed and how can she do that with him? He is no help to her at all. That house on the hill on Fairview is falling apart. She is falling apart!"

The week went fairly well and everyone was getting along including the drunken boyfriend. My partner and I decided to meet his cousin in the city so we drove into town. When we arrived back home that evening, it was apparent that something was really, really wrong. Every light in the big house on the hill was on, all the doors were wide open, and the dog was outside loose and barking. I walked in to find the drunken boyfriend in a rage and my mother was not there. He said he didn't know where she was.

This was the night we were to head back to San Diego. We packed our suitcases while he raged on and we headed out. I called my aunt's house, and that is where my mom was. She told me to come with her there and spend the night. I took my mom to another room and said, "This is it! Enough is enough! You have to make a choice because I can't watch him kill you with stress!" She cried so much and I was so worried she was not going to make it. She was 62 at the time and looked 82.

That night I made a deal with her. If she chose to get rid of him for good, call his kids, and have them take him out of her house, we would move back to Connecticut and help her get the surgeries she needed and put her life back together. We would even help her downsize a bit. Keep in mind she had 40 years' worth of crap in the attic and basement cluttering up her life. She said, "You would leave San Diego?" I said, "You only get one mother and if you are serious about getting rid of him and getting your life back, I would do anything."

We discussed all the way back on the flight from San Diego about moving back. My partner's family was also on the East Coast. 9/11 happened and being close to family seemed like the right thing to do. We discussed the pros and cons and decided to wait and see if she would really get rid of the drunk once and for all.

A week later my mom called crying saying he was gone and left her house a mess. I told her we would be home in February after my graduation from Respiratory School. The entire time one thing was on my mind: how was I going to tell Joey and what was he going to do for someone to depend on? I would take him to his doctor appointments and other things he had on his 'list for Jim' every week.

After graduation I decided it was time to tell Joey what my plan was. I went over to his house and over a joint and a glass of Carlos Rossi I told him the situation. I could see the look of sadness on his face and at the same time the concern about how he was going to do it out there without me around the corner.

Who would have guessed that visiting a guy in the hospital to bring him a few "star rags" would turn into one of the deepest, and most meaningful friendships I have ever experienced in my life? Everything choreographed almost so perfectly that I still question myself, "Was this a dream or reality?" He said, "Well kid, I know when Baha'u'llah calls you and tells you that it's time to move, we may not like it but that is what we have to do. If your mother needs you then you must go and help her." I didn't cry in front of him, but when I got back in my car and drove back over to Kensington Drive to our apartment, I cried about the end of an era. No more painting together listening to America's Song Book, no more laughing watching him laugh watching Springer, and no more smoking joints and having a little red table wine. I knew it would never be the same. Change is difficult, and I knew this would not be an easy transition.

I graduated from Respiratory School with an Associate's Degree. I was the president of my class and gave my speech for a small room of people with Joey and my partner proudly there in the front row. I had already given notice to the managers of the apartment on Kensington Drive. We had several garage sales and downsized to just the basics. We hired UPACK.com/ABF freight and off to Connecticut our stuff was headed.

The day we left San Diego was the most difficult day I had faced in a very long time. I was leaving behind a 20-

year history with a city I loved. A city where I found my heart. A city where I learned the power of faith, healing, and the power of belief. We got to the driveway on 35th street and there was Joey in his neatly pressed bright white t-shirt and jeans. His eyes were filled with sparkle, he had pure snow-white hair and a smile that was so warm and inviting. We said our good-byes as if this was just going to be temporary. I knew it felt different and it was not temporary. He said Allah'u'abha, and I said with tears in my voice Allah'u'abha.

I cried as we pulled away and he was waving. I was so worried about how he was going to survive without me. My Socrates, my mentor, my friend - how would I do without those visits that I so often took for granted?

CHAPTER 12

We arrived in Connecticut to begin our long journey of helping rebuild our lives here. This was the place where I grew up and suddenly knew no one and felt like a foreign visitor in my own town. It was depressing to move from sunny San Diego, the city I loved and adored, back to grey and horrible weather Connecticut. It was like leaving the color of Oz and going back into a depressing black and white movie.

I would call Joey once a week and check in on him, and I knew Bella was doing the same. Her and I developed a phone relationship because she was trying to get Joey to move to Ft. Myers, Florida so he could be near her and her family and she could help keep an eye out for him. Joey was a difficult and stubborn Taurus and was not having it. He really hated Florida, and I think for him it was a sign he was getting old and he felt old people went to Florida to die. He called it Heaven's Waiting Room. "A place for the newly wed and nearly dead," he would say and then laugh.

As the months went on, I could tell he was getting upset knowing that he would have to leave the bungalows on 35th street and head to Florida so he would have more care. He moaned and groaned about the idea of it every time we talked. I would give back to him the story that Baha'u'llah always brings you where you need to be. He still wasn't having it.

Bella called him one day and had it out with him and said, "That is it; we are coming to get you so start packing." I talked with both Bella and Joey and told them about our experience and how inexpensive it was to do UPACK/ABF. Bella and Derrick headed to San Diego. Each week I would talk to Joey it sounded like he was overwhelmed with emptying the garages and getting rid of his "stuff."

He was not talking about packing or getting rid of stuff, he was just complaining how he didn't want to live in Florida and what was he going to do with all his stuff. He knew he would have to move in with Bella and her family until a place opened up at the place at San Piper Run on Ft. Collins Blvd. This became a familiar place for Bella as she took care of her mom there until she passed.

When Bella and Derrick arrived in San Diego, Joey was rare, nasty, rotten attitude Joey. Not typical for him, but when it happened watch out. Bella would argue with him the entire time about getting rid of stuff and taking less. It was painful, but they got both garages empty and off to Florida they went. His stuff would meet them on the other side. He would rent a storage unit in Ft. Myers for his stuff and even rent space and go to the local swap meets to sell his junk. I think he bought more junk for his storage than he sold.

One day I received a call, and it was Joey on the other end. I was so happy to hear his voice! Instead of the normal "Hey kid," it was angry, pissy Joey. I said, "What the hell is wrong?" He said, "Listen, you told me to call that company of yours for moving and they destroyed all my things. Everything is ruined and what do you expect me to do now?" After he was a little calmer, he began to explain that the truck driver of ABF hit something with the top of the cab and all the rain from the trip rained on all of Joeys belongings. He was crushed. He wanted reimbursement and then found they would only give him $0.25 per pound and he would have needed to buy extra moving insurance to cover the costs. It was almost like he was blaming me because I suggested the moving company.

Over the next 18 months he would live with Bella and her husband and oldest son. Joey was not an easy person to live with, especially because he had lived alone the majority of his life and was very set in his ways. Bella and I would begin our secret conversations so she could stay ahead of what was going on. One day I received a call from Bella. She was ripping pissed off to say the least. She was letting the F bombs drop about her frustrations with "My Friend." He was no longer her brother at this point, he was "My Friend."

It seems Joey misplaced some money in his room and made mention to Bella that maybe her son took it. Well watch out when it comes to Bella and her kids. A mama with her cubs. She knew her son would never steal money so Joey must have misplaced it. So, when she called me, she said, "Listen, he needs to get his own place soon because I am tired of all of his bullshit. I have put up with all his ways and him blow drying his balls, but he has done it this time!" I believe the money was found and I think things smoothed over some, but everyone would be happy when Joey's name came up on the list to move him into the Sand Piper Run.

Joey got his place at Sand Piper Run and Derrick was nice enough to give Joey his old red Honda Civic. Joey was happy to have wheels to get to Walmart and to go to his favorite spot at Bunches Beach. Bunches Beach was a place where some gay men would frequent and Joey enjoyed going there and chatting. On occasion, he would meet someone. Old habits die hard as he mentioned on several occasions where he met someone and would bring them back to his place after a day in the sun. Joey never let age stop him, that's for sure.

Joey would find things to do and adjust to life in Ft. Myers. We would talk weekly. He would try to talk me into buying rental units down there so he could live in one and manage the place. He was working so hard to try and recreate what we had at the 35th Street bungalows.

We had started to use South Florida as our playground since we were living on the East Coast. So, we were back and forth to Ft. Lauderdale quite a bit. My partner had spent many of his younger years growing up in Hollywood so it was sort of like a second home. We had lots of fun listening to 80s music and enjoying the resorts and the smell of coconut tanning oil up and down the boardwalk.

On one trip down we rented a car and drove over to Ft. Myers to see Joey and Bella and her family. As always, Bella treated us like she knew us our whole lives. She had a great home with a screened-in pool and a dog named Barbara after Barbara Streisand. Bella loved her gay men. Her best friend in the whole world was her gay friend Louis. He was a business partner, and like a son to her. She was always bragging, "Louis said this and Louis that." It was so wonderful to see that type of love in a friendship.

Joey wanted me to check it out as he was still on this kick about me buying a rental property down in Ft. Myers and that his nephew was so handy and he could "doll a place up" and it would be waiting for us when we were ready to move down. Well, we checked out Ft. Myers and decided we liked South Florida better. It is truly a matter of taste as there are both pluses and minuses on both sides of living in different parts of Florida. Bella loved the whole area around Ft. Myers and Naples. I would never tell Joey directly that I would not be buying a complex that he could manage in Ft. Myers. He really had no concept that I had made the decision to stay in Connecticut for my family and to care for my mother through her older years just as Bella made the commitment to care for both him and their mother.

Joey and I would continue our friendship and conversations over the next few years. He was always hoping in every conversation that I would say we were moving to Ft. Myers. As time went on, I noticed he was slipping a bit here and there. He had made several mistakes and lost his wallet with all his money for the month in it. It just seemed that things were changing for Joey. Even the conversations were starting to become a little foggier. I would start comparing notes with Bella. It came time because of his confusion they had to take the car away. He was upset about the car and would always say he was saving to get another one.

When Joey would get fixated on something, he was on a mission. He saw on the local Ft. Myers TV station a story about a young boy who was being physically abused by the father and the father was in jail and the mother was having to raise two boys on her own. The story became his obsession as the boy was hospitalized from his injury for nine months. Joey continued to follow the story and call the news station to inquire about the boy. Joey could not understand why the news station would not just give him the mother's address so he could go visit and comfort her. After calling the station many times and driving Bella crazy with this, he wanted to bring the boy and his brother matching bikes that he bought them at Walmart. The news station finally contacted the family and they were able to meet Joey at the news station and accept the bikes from Joey as Christmas gifts. He was delighted and so happy to tell me the story. These are the random acts of kindness Joey did before they became trendy. These acts of kindness came from him regardless of which heart he had in him. He said he had always wished he could have met the Marine's family that gave him his heart.

Joey had been asking me if I would please come and visit. I knew my partner was not thrilled with that side of Florida, so I decided to get a cheap hotel and go down and spend a week with Joey. I knew I didn't want to stay with him because I would need my own down time at the end of the day. He wanted to show me around Ft.

Myers and take me to the swap meet and go to the 50s style diner he loved to eat at. I booked myself at the hotel chain's website. When I arrived, I was shocked to see that this place was completely run down and not taken care of. It appeared there were many long-term people living there. I thought this is going to be a long week. Little did I know just how long it would be.

Joey was upset because he thought I would bring along some weed for him. I said, "Joey, no I would never do that and you need to save your lungs these days." I kept making light of it. I knew he wanted the old connection back in the worst way. He wanted some feeling of being the two of us, me laughing and listening to his wonderful colorful stories. I would only see Bella once on this trip and I would later find out it was because she needed a caregiver break. Bella never really explained that she would be taking the week off from him and that I would be doing everything that week, from counting out his pills to listening to him say as I was counting them out, "Isn't this just such a bore? This is what it's come to?" I also took him for his weekly Walmart run.

That is when things went from sad to sadder. I lost him in Walmart or he lost me. Bella had not filled me in on just how bad his dementia was getting. I noticed some in our phone conversations he was a little off but he always recovered well. I lost him for almost an hour, and I was terrified. When I finally found him, he was talking with this young manager. I said, "Hey Joey!" He said, "Oh hey kid, where you been?" I wanted to choke him! I was so upset that I realized the Joey I knew was gone and this was only half of him.

The next day he wanted to show me the swap meet. We went over to the swap meet and it was another day of him wandering off and me losing him. The outings were becoming a huge job for me and I really couldn't wait to go back home. My friend, my mentor, my Socrates, was just barely hanging on. The evening before I left, we met with Bella at a local Italian place he liked. She seemed frazzled and not herself.

When Joey got up from the table to go use the men's room, we had a chance to share notes. She didn't realize that I didn't know he was as bad as he was with his mind. She apologized and thanked me, saying he was driving her nuts and was very demanding and does not realize she still has to work and cannot be there for him on call. Bella and I hugged. I brought Joey back to Sand Piper Run and I knew that he and I had said good bye so many times before but this time would be the last time that I would see my dear friend. We acted as if I would be back soon and did our normal good-bye. He said, "Call me when you get back, Allah'u'abha." I left Ft. Myers and was trying to make peace with everything as well as the realization that as many times as we had done this since we met, this was coming close to the final curtain call.

My plane ride was filled with my silent tears, and I just couldn't wait to get back home.

CHAPTER 13

I had just started my hypnosis practice up in Connecticut and was trying to explain to Joey during one of our phone conversations what I was doing. I knew he always wanted me to be self-employed and a free spirit like he was for so many years. He also told me so many times that I was empathic and a healer and it would take time for me to realize I had "The Gift."

I decided that Christmas to drop my business card in with his Christmas Card. I would usually send him a card with a Pantone Bread, one of his favorites. He received the card and somehow misplaced the business card. Bella called me about a week later. She said, "Help. Do me a favor and send Joey another fuckin' business card before he drives me nuts as he calls me every day asking about it."

Bella and I would check in weekly from this point forward as she knew that Joey was up to something even though he had dementia; she could just sense something was up. One of her first signals was, as she controlled his money, all of a sudden, he was asking for more cash. She said, "Joey, everything is taken care of why do you need more money?" "I just need it," he said. One day he called her and said, "Sis I want you to take me shopping for a pair of slacks and new shoes. I noticed what the new trends are and I would like to see if I could find a decent pair of slacks and nice matching shoes."

I didn't realize he was asking for new clothes from Bella and when she and I began to compare our notes we figured out what Joey had been up to. Apparently on Sunday afternoons he was walking across Ft. Collins Blvd to a gay bar for older men. Keeping in mind his dementia and that it is an 8-lane highway, Baha'u'llah was definitely watching over him!

Bella indeed did take him shopping for his new slacks and shoes. Joey always needed to look and be current with trends. His navy-blue blazer and jeans I guess weren't cutting it for him. It would be the week after she took him shopping that would be the final descent for Joey.

He took too many of his pills by mistake and ended up in rehab. Bella was told she should start to take his apartment down as he would most likely not leave rehab.

She began to clear out his apartment and would call me and tell me what she would find. She said, "Even in a one-bedroom apartment my brother is a hoarder."

Well once again Joey recovered and they said they could not keep him and he needs to go home. When he arrived back home, he saw that Bella had cleaned out a lot of the junk and stuff. He went crazy. He called her and yelled, "Where's my this; where's my that?" She had to go out and buy him a new mattress because she had planned on giving the apartment back. She made sure he had a nurse who would come to supervise his meds as well. He hated it. He called the woman his babysitter and was as miserable as Joey could be when he didn't want or like something.

When we spoke for the last couple of conversations, he was becoming more and more cognitively limited. It wouldn't be long before I would receive the call from Bella telling me that Joey was failing and it didn't look like he was going to make it much longer. I was not very emotional at this point as I felt like he and I had said our good-byes so often, and I had shed so many tears by now that I was already at peace with the inevitable.

Joey got a 20-year bonus with this new heart. His second chance, and he used each day and lived it to the fullest. Bella said on one of the last days she went to see him, he was sitting up, not a hair out of place, and looking great. She said he was sitting on the edge of the bed and he crossed his legs and said, "Hey sis, thanks for coming by." He said, "I just lit a joint; you can join me." He acted as if he had a joint in his hand and passed it to her. She told me she pretended to take a hit from it and hand it back. He said, "No, it's ok sis, hit it again." She played along.

The following day she received the call. Joey made his final transition to the next life. He was now with Baha'u'llah. His journey was complete. All the lessons he needed to share - completed. Mission accomplished. Bella called me to give me the news. I felt bad because the tears I was shedding were for her and the loss of her brother and companion. Her life was going to be changed forever now that he was gone. She was so upset because she knew Joey was Bahai and that he wanted to be buried in a mausoleum. He never wanted to be cremated and at the same time in true Joey fashion he thought someone else would take care of it. Bella certainly didn't have the financial means to purchase a mausoleum. Joey was cremated.

Bella called me and invited me to meet her in Lake Merrit to sprinkle Joey's ashes near the house they rented and spent so much time at water skiing. She would do this on the one-year anniversary of his transition to the next life. She also released balloons. When she and her friends arrived in Lake Merritt they were concerned because there is never any parking available. In true Joey Romain style, they pulled up in front of the house that they had rented at Lake Merritt and the car that was parked in front of it pulled away giving them an open spot right in front of the house. She said it was a glorious day. Perfect weather when she sprinkled the ashes. She would do the same at Bunches Beach in Ft. Myers and they release balloons there every year on his anniversary and birthday.

The following year Bella was planning on coming up to see her friend Franny in Poughkeepsie. She so wanted to meet us for lunch. Bella and Fran drove from Poughkeepsie just to have lunch with my partner and I. We had the most charming lunch with them. Fran told the story about when she flew down to Florida to take Joey to see Johnny Matthis. He loved Johnny Matthis. When Fran arrived, he took one look at her and said, "Girl, don't you have a mirror? What's wrong with your hair? It looks like the rats spent the winter in it." He laughed and she was hysterical because she knew Joey since they were kids and said, "That's him." No filter and when it came to hair Joey expected everyone's hair to be perfect just like his was up until the day he passed on.

At lunch Bella gave me the initial ring that Joey always wore, JR. She also gave me one of the few pictures that I have of Joey and me standing outside of Point Loma Sea Food out on Point Loma in San Diego. I want you to have these things as I know Joey treasured your friendship and would want you to have them. We said our good-byes and talked about us coming down for a visit soon. We were sincere as we wanted to get down to see them. Well, we finally did. I was so happy we got to see them and I always loved the moments we could share Romain stories and laugh.

Life is filled with twists and turns and even as I write the final words in the book, I know that I was divinely guided to "tell the story" just as he would have wanted it told. Have the faith and believe with the excitement and expectancy that it is coming. All you need is the faith, healing, and the power of belief!

FINAL NOTE

December 26, 2020

It was Christmas Day. The last thing I had in mind was finishing the last part of this book before the other chapters had even been written. Due to the pandemic and a myriad of other issues, it didn't feel like the holiday season at all. It felt as if everyone was just going through the motions. I was on the phone wishing my father a Merry Christmas when a call came in from Ft. Myers, Florida. The only person I knew in Ft. Myers was Joey's sister Bella, and I had her number programmed in my phone. Not recognizing the number, I let it go to voicemail. The same number came in again, but I also let it go to voicemail. When I was done talking with my father, I played the message back.

I heard Bella's husband Derrick's voice, "If this is Jim, Joey's friend, this is Bella's husband Derrick. Can you call me back please?" I immediately knew it could not be good news.

My initial gut feeling turned out to be my worst fear; on December 23, 2020, Bella made her transition suddenly by cardiac arrest to Baha'u'llah and to be with Joey in the place that he always said was better than anything we could ever dream or imagine.

It's as if I was grieving the loss of my friend Joey again. There was no more mutual connection with anyone that knew Joey. I realize now her friendship with me kept Joey alive for me. I never really had to grieve him totally because she and I would reminisce by the hour about him and his ways of looking at life. We always said the world could be blowing up around Joey and he would always remain calm, cool, and collected no matter what was going wrong. He was like Mr. Magoo, not only behind the wheel of a car, but in life itself. He also had a very Winnie-the-Pooh attitude that all would be ok, and there is really nothing to worry about. Bella being gone is truly the last chapter of "the story." Her and Joey are together now. He always said Baha'u'llah is in charge, and he will bring you where he wants you.

It is now time for you to have the same faith and belief that Joey had! Whatever it is you are waiting for, it is coming. You are worthy and deserving of receiving it, and all you have to do is have the belief that it's on its way. Because now you understand about the faith, healing, and the power of belief.

Alwad u adha!

1. Relationships- They come and go. Some people are in your life for a short time and others for a lifetime.

2. Debt- A loss of freedom that you create and have complete control over. You sell hours of your life ahead of time when you create debt and you have to get out of bed more to pay them back.

3. Know that you are enough just the way you are.

4. Always leave anything you buy or rent better than the way you found it. Paint works wonders so "doll things up."

5. Work out and take care of your body. No one likes fat, neither the person who is fat nor the person that has to be underneath you. BACK AWAY FROM THE TABLE AND LOOK IN THE MIRROR! Nothing grows in the shade except mushrooms.

6. Presentation matters. Always present your best and look your best when going out. Presentation is everything.

7. Never fear being broke because you can count on Baha'u'llah to fill up your bank account with all that you need.

8. He believed as a Bahai that you should always give back financially to your faith.

9. Regardless of your age, you can always just put on a cowboy hat, a pair of mirrored sunglasses, and a towel, and you are hot no matter what your age is. There is someone for everyone. Only go out when you feel like you can strut like a peacock and make sure it is a day you feel really good about yourself.

10. Ask Baha'u'llah for what you need, not what you want. He knows when you need a heart and you will get one if you ask. When you ask, have faith in him that if you have the desire, the belief, and the EXPECTATION, then Baha'u'llah will bring you more than you could have ever imagined.

ABOUT THE AUTHOR

James M. Vera is America's Leading Inspirational Hypnotist. At an early age he was influenced by great inspirational speakers such as Leo Buscaglia, Dr. Wayne Dyer, Louise Hay, and Dr. Joe Vitale to name a few that made a permanent lasting impression on his life. James likes to deliver his message with a sense of humor and a dose of reality. He continues to share all his insights as both a private coach as well as an inspirational keynote speaker for all types of groups and organizations. James has helped countless people through his speaking engagements, books, and private coaching to know that once they make the choice to change the rest is easy. Like his mentors mentioned above, he believes that love is the healer and it all begins with belief. He is also the author of *Hypnoketosis: Eat the Foods You Love and Lose Weight While You Sleep.*

www.ingramcontent.com/pod-product-compliance
Lightning Source LLC
Chambersburg PA
CBHW061735050726
47598CB00002B/489